Olivia Holmes
Meets
Luke and Alice

MARK DAYDY

ISBN: 9798529328927

Cover design by MIKE DAYDY

CONTENTS

Prologue

Thirty-six years ago…

Olivia Holmes was nine years old. An age when playing outside with friends topped her list of the most important things to do during the school holidays.

However, despite it being a fabulously sunny August day, she was spending time with her parents in a pub in the middle of nowhere. Worse still, she was nursing an almost empty glass of lemonade while the grown-ups talked about things like house prices and gridlocked roads.

A lady called Gloria seemed to be important. She had a thin face and hair that never moved. Obviously, a user of firm hold hairspray like in the TV ads. Mum said windy days turned Olivia's hair into an abandoned bird's nest. Perhaps firm hold hairspray was the answer?

Olivia liked Gloria's pale blue dress. It made her look like a piece of summer sky floating around to cheer people up. Most people didn't seem very cheered up though – even when Gloria stopped to talk to them about wine.

"Try this one," said a man with a penknife that turned

1

into a corkscrew.

He opened a bottle of white wine and passed it their way.

Olivia's dad duly sniffed the contents, as did Olivia's mum. Olivia got involved too, sniffing the open neck.

The wine's *bouquet,* as Dad called it, reminded her of…

Sweaty armpits.

Mum and Dad poured a little into their glasses and sniffed again. Olivia surreptitiously placed a hand over her lemonade glass, just in case. Meanwhile, Gloria came over and made comments about the bouquet that didn't make sense.

Roses. Bananas. Lemons.

No mention of armpits.

"Alice!" the penknife man called out.

Olivia looked across the pub to pinpoint Alice – a young woman who collected a tray of fresh glasses from the bar and brought them over. She had lovely pink streaks in her hair.

Olivia instantly decided that she'd like to have pink streaks when she grew up.

Meanwhile, descriptions of the bouquet continued.

Grapefruit. Chalk. Pear drops.

Olivia had the idea of sniffing the remnants of her lemonade.

Sugar. Not much lemon.

She looked to her parents, who sipped the wine and smiled at Gloria in a way that avoided saying yuck, this is horrible.

Olivia smiled too, but she couldn't understand why they had come. They didn't belong here.

1

Who's in Charge?

The Present Day

"It's going to be a glorious summer," yelled Olivia Holmes, "and we're going to enjoy it together because the Fates have decreed it!"

She eyeballed a panting dog some fifty yards away by the old stone bridge. They seemed to have different ideas about who was in charge.

"Bella? Are you listening? I'm sure the Fates meant to give me a clever, well-trained dog. So, come here!"

Bella remained rooted to the spot – her tongue hanging out sideways in much the same way Olivia's had thirty-six years earlier when she portrayed a murder victim in the school play.

"Okay, stay there then."

Bella watched her owner cover forty-eight yards before turning and running off, tail wagging, to explore beyond the short, narrow, single arch bridge.

Olivia came to halt by the 'Bridge Closed' sign attached to a concrete barrier. According to Ken it had been there for the past five years, blocking access for vehicles – although not for pedestrians, cyclists, or runaway dogs.

Poor old Ken. His friend Milly Ramsey passed away at the beginning of April. A sudden loss due to her heart giving out. Eight weeks on, Ken was doing his best to get back to normal – or at least give that impression outwardly. Olivia had spotted him a couple of times loitering on the corner of Frampton Lane where Milly had lived.

It was now the end of May – eighteen months since Olivia first set foot in Jo the solicitor's office to meet her cousins Sue and Milo... and to discover that they had inherited something unusual.

She glanced up at the sky – mostly blue but with rain clouds gathering. She was ready for it thanks to a proper waxed raincoat and sensible shoes. Weather was important in the countryside.

She recalled her early adventures along the footpath by the fields opposite the top end of Colshot Lane. Back then, among the wildflowers, she took photos because this place was coming to mean something to her.

Now she would often walk down Colshot Lane in the other direction, around the bend to the left, and take a right turn into Potter's Lane – which led to the bridge. It was farther to go, but it was worth the effort.

Naturally, she still took photos. It was just that now they all seemed to feature a mischievous one-year-old crossbreed Alsatian – or half-satian as Olivia preferred.

She checked her watch. It wasn't quite six o'clock, meaning the meeting in the village was just over an hour away. Plenty of time for Bella to let off steam.

Two small birds flashed by.

Goldfinches?

How peaceful it was.

It was a shame the bridge was due to be demolished.

She didn't agree with it, but she understood. This old stone affair had served the community since the days of horses and carts moving between Maybrook and Ralston and farther afield. According to a metal plaque attached to one side of the bridge, its construction dated back to 1867.

She imagined it – like a scene from a novel by one of the Brontë sisters… clattering wheels on cobblestone… only the scene morphed into hatchback cars, box vans and articulated trucks roaring across a modern, two-lane replacement bridge.

According to Gus, the planners felt the old bridge was about as useful as an ashtray on a motorbike – or, in admin-speak, that the soon-to-be-constructed Forest Edge housing development, a hundred yards up on the other side, required vehicular access to the village.

Gus…

They had been together since the harvest seven months ago and were getting along very nicely. Nights out, nights in, occasional sleepovers at his or hers…

Olivia of old would have told him she loved him around February and invited him to move in with her around… well, February.

But the new, measured Olivia had learned from past mistakes.

No more rushing in.

So…?

Summer was almost upon them and Measured Olivia's smug maturity was beginning to annoy Original Olivia. While Gus came across as happy to continue as they were, he also seemed ready to take things to the next level.

If she were any judge of character…

She stopped that line of thought and patted the stone

wall. Below, the lively Hanway stream bubbled on its way to meet May's Brook a mile west of the village.

Looking up from the water, she spotted a family on the bank a fair way downstream – two adults and a small child. They were pointing at things and no doubt discussing every sighting. Something so simple and yet so wonderful. Somewhere deep in her soul she felt that familiar yearning for what might have been.

Jamie…

Parenthood wasn't a gift bestowed on everyone.

It *had* been bestowed on Gus though. That was something she learned during those weeks following the harvest – that he had a fourteen-year-old son called Luke who lived with an aunt in Maidstone and liked music, art, and disagreeing with adults.

Luke, now fifteen, would be in Maybrook tomorrow. It was the half-term holiday and he'd decided on a Friday lunchtime visit. Olivia was looking forward to it, but perhaps with some trepidation. Luke had only visited Gus twice in the past year and neither time had she set eyes on him. Gus meanwhile visited him every couple of months, but it was hard to tell what kind of relationship they had.

All she knew was that Gus's relationship with a woman called Melanie ended when Luke was nine. He took her surname, Collingwood. Alas, Melanie died three years later from cervical cancer and Luke went to live with his mum's sister, Beth. He'd had the option to live with Gus but had chosen not to take it.

Bella?

Her dog was on the bank below the bridge.

"Don't go in the water," she called.

Bella was a rescued mutt – not ill-treated, but too much for a couple with small children who thought Bella would complete their joy.

She didn't.

They hadn't called her Bella either, but Hashtag.

Bella was Olivia's idea. A new name for a new beginning – and what better place than Whitman Farm for new beginnings.

"Bella! Stay!"

Bella paused and stared. And then moved off again.

"Who's in charge here?" Olivia demanded.

Bella responded by rolling in the mud.

Great…

Olivia raised her arm as if to throw.

"Bella, fetch!"

Momentarily having the dog's attention, she aimed an imaginary twig along the bank – and watched Bella assume it had landed in the stream.

"Bella, leave!"

Bella moved to the edge and placed a hesitant paw in the water. Olivia hurried across the bridge and down onto the bank. She didn't want a soggy dog. What she wanted was…

Her left foot landed on a squelchy tuft – which broke free, surfboard-like, towards the water.

"Arggh-arhh!" she cried as she performed the splits and slammed into the bubbling Hanway.

Bella took this to mean, "The water's lovely, come on in!"

Olivia stood up in six inches of ice-cold water and shivered. Her only dry item of clothing was the waxed raincoat from which the water ran off beautifully like in some perverse TV ad. Worse still, judging by the noxious stench, her dog hadn't rolled in mud.

"Bella, get out!" she barked.

Bella barked back. This was evidently a better game than Retrieve the Imaginary Stick, which was no longer retrievable due to it floating away downstream.

Five minutes later, as they reached the junction of Potter's Lane and Colshot Lane, a slightly built, hawk-like local man paused to study them. Old Roper, Ken called him. No doubt he was on his way to meet like-minded village elder Alan Curtis-Fisher who lived a little farther on. Both gave the impression they had served Maybrook long enough to deserve a statue.

"How's London?" he asked.

"Haven't been there in ages," said Olivia, determined to repel the role of newcomer.

"Right… so… looks like we might have rain."

"Yes, but what's a little rain…" *compared with a swim.*

"Was it raining where you've been?" Old Roper asked.

Olivia could see the suspicion in his eyes. Perhaps this wasn't the time to mention she'd be seeing him again at the meeting in an hour.

"Rain? No," she said before striding off with her dignity undermined by socks and shoes that squelched with cartoon sound effects.

2

Getting Ready

Olivia felt at home at Whitman Farm. She really did. Despite being the soggy owner of an untrained reeking mutt, she smiled as they came up the front path to the house, recalling the first time she set eyes on the place – a rundown old property with bay windows either side of a central door, badly flaking paint, broken glass panes, missing roof tiles, a jungle of weeds, a collapsed front fence...

It was in much better condition now. The roof was in order with a number of tiles replaced and the flashing against the chimney fixed. The wooden windows had been repaired and painted white, the oak front door was resplendent in deep crimson gloss with a polished brass doorknob, and the front garden had been tamed.

She had never felt this way with her London apartment, but that was life, she supposed. Sometimes, someone, somewhere would be bumbling along aimlessly, and Fate would strike with an indiscriminate bolt of good fortune.

There was no rhyme or reason – just random luck. And that was fine by Olivia Holmes.

Entering the house, she could imagine Gloria coming down the stairs. And Charlie standing in the lounge doorway. Somewhere out the back would be Gloria's parents and grandparents. She had developed a feeling for Whitman Farm's history. There were photos on the wall these days. She was sure there would be more. They wouldn't be forgotten.

A few moments later at the upstairs landing's airing cupboard, she grabbed three of Bella's towels and headed into the bathroom. Nonchalance was the word.

Bella followed…

Slam!

"A nice bath, doggie?"

Olivia opened the taps to get a couple of inches in the tub – enough to give muddy paws a good soak.

Bella looked doubtful.

"Hey, it's okay, we've got Woof Bubbles for a shiny coat."

Bella began to quake.

"What's that, Bella? You'd prefer a large brandy? Well, it's your own fault for rolling in the dung of Lucifer."

A few moments later, Olivia put a trembling canine wreck into the tub and ran the shower attachment over her.

This was not appreciated.

*

Thirty minutes later, a clean owner and super-shiny dog came downstairs ready to face the rest of the day.

In the hall, Olivia paused to glance in the long mirror. Her auburn locks were not entirely auburn these days but looked good in a short cut. Pleasingly, her hazel eyes shone brighter than ever, and her once round face was a lot less round. With a local meeting to attend a little later, a lightweight blue sweater over charcoal chinos looked just about right.

In the lounge, while Bella rolled around on the rug, possibly in an attempt to remove the unacceptable whiff of Woof Bubbles, Olivia googled dog training on her phone. Moments later, she was viewing a website chock full of videos, blogs, and advice.

"Intense training… yes, I think we'll have a go at that."

She eyed Bella.

"Poor doggy, it's not your day, is it. First, fur-washing, now brainwashing."

She studied the introductory questions, the first of which was, 'Is your dog a good canine citizen?'

She addressed Bella directly.

"Are you a good canine citizen?"

Bella sat up and Olivia continued the grilling.

"Do you bark at delivery drivers? Or drag your owner along the street during walks? Are you well behaved around other dogs?"

Bella walked away.

"We're going to use positive reinforcement, Bella. That means a real commitment. There are no shortcuts. Training is built on the relationship between the two of us. And remember – it's fun."

Bella flopped down by the sofa and seemed to sigh.

Olivia smiled sympathetically.

"Then again, maybe you don't need training. Maybe you're—"

The doorbell rang – and Bella launched herself past Olivia, out of the lounge, into the hall, and paws-first at the front door, causing the county of Kent to shake.

"It's only me," an elderly male voice called from

outside.

Bella's joy went off the scale as Olivia squeezed past her to open the door.

"Hello Ke—" was all she got out before her dog jumped all over him.

Ken managed to stay on his feet and took it in good heart.

"How's dog ownership going?" he asked.

"Sorry, Ken. Come in. I'm nearly ready. Is Beano on guard duty?"

"Yes, if he can tear himself away from his jumbo chew."

They were going to the monthly parish council meeting – part of Olivia's plan to gradually integrate herself into the wider community.

"Enjoy your walk?" Ken asked as he followed her into the lounge. "I saw you heading down the lane."

"We went over the bridge. It's so lovely there." She wouldn't be mentioning her impromptu swim.

"It might come up at the meeting," said Ken. "There's an item about new housing developments."

"Interesting – although the bridge's fate seems settled."

"Do you know we used to have a village postcard? It was a montage of views. That bridge was one of them."

"I'm wondering if they've looked into it properly."

Olivia sat down to put her shoes on. Bella seized the opportunity to leap onto her lap.

"She seems right at home," said Ken.

"Yes, I'll just remove her from my personal space and get these laces tied."

"Changing the subject…"

"Please do."

"Have you thought about going to wine classes?"

"Wine classes?" Olivia eased Bella off her lap. "Once or twice. I mean I keep thinking it's the next step, but…"

"There's a course starting next week at the Hallam Hotel. You drive down Southway and follow it a few miles until you join the coast road. Turn right and it's up on the left."

"Yes, I've heard of it."

"It runs for eight Wednesday evenings, and you get a certificate."

"Ooh, I could impress people."

"They have further classes you can take. If you're serious."

"I *am* serious. I did actually do some basic tasting a while back."

"Oh? You never said."

"It was with a friend of mine. Cass. We… well, mainly me… small bottles. I don't recall much else."

"This is a proper Level Two course. Although I'm sure it's fun too."

"What happened to Level One?"

"That's three evenings of entertainment for people who know absolutely nothing. It's really not my area, but I'd say you'd be perfect for Level Two."

"Eight evenings… perhaps you could come with me, Ken."

She was thinking of all the spare evenings he had now that Milly was gone.

"No, this is your territory," he said. "So, Level Two is eight weeks, Level Three is sixteen, and Level Four is sixty spread over two years."

"That's quite a commitment."

"It's not for the uncommitted, that's for sure."

"Well, I'm up for it. I've been lucky to get this chance thanks to Gloria. I want to build on it."

"Indeed."

Olivia wondered about something.

"Do you ever think about luck, Ken? There I am, bumbling along, and wham! Fate and fortune step in."

"They're certainly forces in all our lives."

The doorbell rang and Bella once more set off like a rocket. A moment later, with Olivia finally getting a chance to fasten her shoelaces, Ken and Bella showed Sue into the lounge.

"Cam's not coming," she said.

"I don't blame him," said Ken.

Olivia nodded. She knew that Cam had attended enough parish council meetings for one lifetime – a legacy of his time as a council member.

"Parish councillors…" said Ken, who had himself been one for most of the 1980s and 90s. "There are one or two I'd swear belong to the Mafia. If you had two backs, they'd stab you in both of them."

"Let's not upset them then," said Olivia, rising to her feet.

3

The Meeting

Maybrook Village Hall sat alongside the graveyard behind St Mary's Church. It was built in 1951 to coincide with the Festival of Britain – that national celebration of fresh ideas designed to ignite an exciting post-War future. That said, where the Festival on London's South Bank embraced modernism with a Dome of Discovery and a Space Age 'floating' Skylon, Maybrook's elders opted for a mock-Tudor cabin.

In fairness, it was a clean and airy shelter whose 100 seats were regularly folded away to make room for social functions and a children's playgroup. And every summer, its exterior boasted hanging baskets bursting with begonias, fuchsias, petunias, geraniums and lobelia – courtesy of a small group of volunteers which now included the recently-retired Sue.

Since its creation, the village hall had hosted hundreds of parish council meetings. This would be Olivia's third. Both previous meetings had been dull, but she was keen to take the small steps needed to become part of the wider community. She didn't want to simply reside in Maybrook, she wanted to belong.

That said, the chairs were hard – perhaps to deter people from settling in for an evening of hurling tough questions at the council. After twenty minutes, a substantial majority would definitely be thinking of moving on to the pub.

No, she would ignore the discomfort. It was a matter of being seen as the woman from the vineyard who took a respectful interest in the way the village was run. With three new housing developments due to be discussed, she was hoping a council member might bring up the subject of the old stone bridge. If they didn't, perhaps a member of the public would.

Sitting alongside Ken and Sue, she recognised most of the two dozen or so other attendees, although she didn't know any of them personally. Neither did she know particularly well any of the eight council members – among them the smart, silver-haired chairman, Alan Curtis-Fisher, who lived in Colshot Lane around the bend past Cam's brother's place.

"Order! Order! I declare this meeting open," said Mr Curtis-Fisher. "Item One, the roadside welcome signs that greet drivers entering the village. They're getting old."

"Aren't we all," declared an elderly voice in the audience.

"None of us are getting any younger," added another.

"The question is," said the chairman, "should they be restored or replaced?"

"The welcome signs or the old people?"

After a short debate, a decision was deferred pending a costing exercise.

"Item Two – the public bench outside the church, put

there in 1988 but used less and less due to its proximity to the ever-busier road. It's due to be replaced, but the question is – should the new one be located elsewhere?"

Again, following a short discussion, a decision was deferred pending a costing exercise.

Item Three included a brief progress report on the Forest Edge housing development. Naturally, concerns were raised over policies on schools and healthcare, although it was pointed out that these were weightier matters to be dealt with at a higher tier of local authority. Where the parish council could get involved would be in providing guidance as to impact. With this in mind, the debate moved on to traffic and, finally, to replacing the bridge.

"Without a new bridge," said Alan Curtis-Fisher, "people living at Forest Edge will drive the other way to Ralston. Maybrook is nearer as the crow flies but it won't be crows living there."

"There's only one store in Ralston," said a member of the public.

"Yes, but it sells everything," said another. "Do you know I was able to get purple bootlaces there?"

"Purple?" said a third. "What about cake tins?"

Alan Curtis-Fisher cut in.

"We must get the people who move into Forest Edge to spend time and money in Maybrook."

"Too right," said Old Roper from a seat directly behind Olivia, provoking her into wondering when he'd last taken a bath. "It's only 897 yards from Forest Edge to the near end of the High Street."

"That's very precise," said another member of the public.

"I measured it."

"How?"

"With footsteps."

Olivia closed her eyes. She wasn't troubled by who was speaking now.

"Why didn't you use one of those little wheels on a stick?"

"No need. I know my stride length."

"I can get you a wheel on a stick. The district council has a spare one."

"I've already measured it. I've also just finished painting my back door yellow. Next you'll be telling me you know a place that sells yellow paint."

"That place in Ralston sells yellow paint. And doors."

Olivia quietened her mind while the discussion rumbled on for another minute or so.

"The main thing," Alan Curtis-Fisher eventually said to restore order, "is that the parish council supports the new bridge."

"Well, you would," said a member of the public. "Morgan Fairfax are paying for it."

"Most of it," another audience member interjected. "The taxpayer's still expected to contribute."

Olivia, aware that Morgan Fairfax Properties were behind the Forest Edge development, raised her hand.

"Couldn't they find another way to link Forest Edge with the main road?"

Alan Curtis-Fisher bristled.

"You mean create a new road through the forest? Disturbing all the nature thereabouts?"

Olivia was taken aback.

"I was only wondering if there might be an alternative to a new bridge."

"You're from the vineyard, aren't you?"

"Focusing on the old bridge," said another council member, a woman possibly in her mid-fifties, "we welcome all opinions."

Olivia nodded in gratitude and felt confident enough to continue.

"Isn't there an existing lane through the forest that could be improved?"

"No," said Old Roper from behind her. "No such lane or way exists. Never has, never will. Not over my dead body."

From the platform, Alan Curtis-Fisher sniffed as he eyed Olivia.

"If you get time, I suggest you take a proper look at what's what. There's no chance we'd build a road through the forest. I'm sure I have the consent of the hall to say that."

A murmur confirmed it.

"I can assure you, I never meant…" but Olivia gave up. Ken leaned in close.

"Another thirty years and they'll accept you as a villager."

Olivia sighed.

"Anyway," said Alan Curtis-Fisher, "you'll be a beneficiary."

"Me?" Olivia didn't understand.

"We'll widen the road south from the new development, put the new bridge in, widen Potter's Lane, turn left into Colshot Lane, which we'll widen for a short stretch. Then, where it bends round to your place, we'll continue straight on instead, with a new stretch of road fifty yards across common land to the main road. Your part of Colshot Lane will be blocked off from the traffic. You should be pleased."

"I never knew," said Olivia.

"Me neither," said Ken.

"Nor would you," said Alan Curtis-Fisher. "These are

just my thoughts, which I intend to discuss with the developer and the district council. Now, if there are no further suggestions, we'll move onto Item Four. The space between the rear of the Old Hall and the school is looking sad. We need to improve the flower beds…"

*

After the parish council's business had been concluded, Olivia wondered if Ken was a good citizen for attending every meeting or whether he just liked to keep an eye on them.

As it was, Ken introduced her to the council member who had welcomed all opinions – Katy Law, who was now with her elderly dad, Steve.

"Thanks for raising a hand," said Katy. "We need people taking an active interest."

"No problem," said Olivia.

"I'm wondering if the bridge might be a road safety issue," said Steve. "Maybrook hasn't always been safe for cyclists. Do you remember that incident, Ken?"

Ken thought for a moment.

"I do, Steve. It was way back though. I doubt it would help a fresh road safety campaign. Not after all this time."

"You're probably right," said Steve.

"I must say hello to someone," said Ken.

Having spotted a friend, he left them to it.

"So, what happened?" Olivia asked Steve.

"Oh… a young woman lost her life. Ken's right though. It was a long time ago – thirty years or more. It wouldn't help much with a fresh campaign."

"You might be on to something though," said Katy. "The area beyond Forest Edge is earmarked for further development. That'll mean growing numbers walking and cycling over the bridge. We want the best outcome, not a rushed decision."

"I'm sure it'll be perfectly safe," said Olivia, "but I do sometimes wonder why progress always seems to mean losing something."

"I'll email someone I know," said Katy. "I might be able to buy you a little more time."

Olivia smiled weakly.

Me…?

4

The Luke Factor

On Friday morning, with secateurs, heavy-duty gloves, and a dog, Olivia made her way through Whitman Farm's flourishing vines of mainly Chardonnay, pinot noir, and pinot Meunier. With sparkling wine in mind, this was the business's future.

Thankfully, the wires that took the weight of the fruit and canopy were covered by the glorious natural look of a vineyard on the cusp of summer. And the alleys were a treat too – busy now with lively displays of daisies, buttercups, bugles, eggs and bacon, and sneezewort.

Olivia's second winter hadn't been as tough as the first. Paying local agricultural workers to help with the pruning between December and February had made a big difference – especially to her ankles, knees and back.

By the end of the first year, she had learned a lot. But now, deep into Year Two, she was pushing on, reading up on nutrition, disease control, and canopy management – although learning a fuller range of poems, songs, and dances to cover all situations had yet to materialize.

She looked up at the sky. A little rain later wouldn't do any harm to the micro-clusters of flowers now appearing. Micro-clusters were a big thing in Year One. They were today, too. They always would be.

"We're doing well," she told Bella.

What had Ken said that first time? That he liked to see flowering? He'd said it while looking at Olivia not the vines.

Yes, she had the passion for this.

Gus often said he liked her passion for her new life. He'd told her many times she was the real deal. Sometimes she felt it was quite something to live up to. That said, she couldn't imagine being stuck in an office. How many people had worked here in the open air? Not just among the vines but going back to Whitman Farm's first days…?

Heading for the nature reserve at the rear of the vineyard, she planned to finally commence an attack on its rampant weeds and bramble. The reserve was the area Charlie had set aside years ago to encourage and observe wildlife. Hence the slatted wooden bench that would be a great place to sit and read in solitude, and simply blend into a landscape she increasingly felt she belonged to.

Picking her way through the entanglement to reach Whitman's Farm's rear boundary, she came to a fence of rotten wooden stakes strung with broken chicken wire. This separated them from the cereal farmland owned by a company called Moorcroft's, who operated from a farmhouse and outbuildings way over on the far side.

It was a wonderful, open expanse with a big sky overhead. Somewhere distant, a crow arrk-arrked.

"Mmm, the sounds of the countryside…"

Her phone pinged.

It was a text from Gus.

'All set for lunch?'

Lunch was hours away, but, yes, she was ready. It was going to be a total success.

*

Olivia glanced at the kitchen clock. It was a few minutes past noon. Luke would soon be arriving at Gus's place where he and his dad would have a cheery catch-up. Then they would stroll round to her place for lunch. Gus had been useless; unable to answer simple questions as to what kind of sandwich or juice Luke would like. She ended up buying enough options to feed a football team.

Still, it would be fun – that was the main thing.

She laid a new white tablecloth and set out the plates, cutlery, glasses, cups, and crimson paper serviettes.

And lunch itself? She checked the fridge. It was all prepared and ready to eat. Potato salad, quiche Lorraine, honey-glazed ham, Somerset cheddar cheese, Moroccan couscous, red pepper humus, Italian mixed leaves, spring onions, celery sticks, cherry tomatoes, coleslaw, orange juice, apple juice, lemonade, cola, and bottled water.

She closed the fridge and surveyed the scene.

Bread…?

She took three small French baguettes from the paper bag on the worktop and placed them on a plate in the middle of the table.

Floor vacuumed?

Check.

Everywhere super-tidied and polished to death?

Check.

She wondered about that. Was it wise to show Luke a level of trouble that she rarely went to under normal circumstances? Wasn't this a misrepresentation of the relaxed person she was – or at least aspired to be?

No, this was just her helping Gus to make a success of Luke's visit. It would be appreciated.

All she needed to do was check in with the Fates, the Universe, the Great Unknown – after all, these higher forces had a recent track record of bringing her good fortune.

O Great Universal Power, is there anything I've missed?

Her phone pinged.

The Great Universal Power sends texts…?

It was Gus.

'Not heard from Luke. Have texted him x'

Olivia starred at the screen. Was Luke okay? He was coming by bus. It was daft to worry, of course. He'd show up soon enough. How to handle him – that was the real question. He could end up being her…

No…

No, she was getting ahead of herself.

For a moment, she imagined it was Jamie coming to lunch. She would have given the earth for that. And her right arm. And the vineyard.

Focus, woman, focus!

She went through to the lounge. It was shaping up nicely. The photos helped. Not just the one of Gloria in her bathing suit. There were others now. One of Charlie with a golden retriever called Ruby pleased her.

"Whitman Farm has to have a dog," she said.

Bella came in and yawned.

"Ken says there's very likely been a dog here since the farm began. I think he meant a working dog though. I don't think you qualify."

Bella came over and nuzzled her hand. It was a marked difference to their first meeting where Bella, or Hashtag, looked depressed at the dogs' home.

"It's okay," said Olivia. "You belong here now."

Yes, she had her dog. They would be great together. Olivia and Bella. It was just a matter of evolving out of their Laurel and Hardy phase.

She eyed Sue and Cam's wedding invitation on the mantlepiece and smiled. That would be a fine day come the end of July. Those two already behaved as if they'd been married thirty years. It wouldn't be a big white wedding – more a low-key blessing. Cam's brother would be best man. Olivia would be maid of honour.

As for her own relationship arrangements, the time was fast-approaching when she would ask Gus to move out of the terrible bachelor pad above his garage and into the house at Whitman Farm. In the spirit of making any transition easy for him, she'd already made some changes – such as ensuring the bookcase was quite blatantly only half full.

So, Luke? To worry or not to worry?

It was an hour before Gus texted again.

'Luke not coming. Had stuff to deal with. He'll come for Sunday lunch. Back to work for me x'

Olivia groaned. But what did she expect? Luke wasn't to know she'd made an effort. He didn't even know he was meant to accompany Gus to her house. Gus's intention had been to introduce the idea casually. A 'thrown together' lunch. No big deal. No fuss. Apparently, Luke didn't like a fuss.

She liberated a piece of quiche from the fridge and wondered if Whitman Farm would be a family home again anytime soon. A few minutes later, she put everything away, grabbed her gloves, and went back out to the vineyard, to her real life.

5

Alice

That evening, Olivia and Sue headed for the Royal Standard – their first girls' night out in ages. They walked there with Ken, who seemed keen to discuss seasonal fruit, the gulf stream's influence on British weather, and unusual boats.

At the pub, he was first to the door and, like a gentleman, he held it open for Olivia and Sue... so that they were first to enter and first to the bar.

It was fairly busy inside with the hubbub of half a dozen conversations. Ted and Tom, two of Ken's old friends greeted them from a corner table.

"Hello ladies, hello Ken," said Ted. "Some men have all the luck."

"Just my usual for me," Ken advised Olivia before going over to the modest stage to say hello to Folkie-Karaoke – violinist Gus, guitarist Killy and accordionist Harpo – who were setting up for an evening of turning pop songs into folk classics.

Gus waved to Olivia and Sue before greeting Ken. Olivia smiled. She loved the feeling of it being their pub, their village, and would happily have done this more often. It was just that Sue and Cam liked nothing better than spending a hundred consecutive evenings at home. Currently, poor old Cam was with his brother, Tony, probably trying to remember how to spend an evening with someone else.

That said, there would be plenty of opportunities for Sue and Cam to dance to Folkie-Karaoke at the end of July, when the band were booked to play at their wedding reception.

At the bar, landlady Annie's nephew, Dave welcomed them – Annie herself having gone to stay with her sister at the coast for a few days.

While being served a couple of gin and tonics and Ken's glass of red, Olivia pondered the Gus and Luke situation. Or, more accurately, the Gus situation. Luke was obviously a figment of his imagination.

No, that was unfair. And she guessed she was the last person to think something like that.

She wondered – if they ever got into a permanent relationship would she share how she still occasionally talked to Jamie – or at least talked to who Jamie might have become.

Probably not.

She and Sue were soon seated – too close to Ted though, who leaned across from the adjacent table.

"I hear you caused a few ripples last night. Questions about the old bridge."

"I only asked if we could save it," said Olivia.

Ted nodded. "Maybe make it a road safety issue?"

"You've been talking to Steve and Katy."

Tom nudged Ted. "You've been found out, mate."

"Nonsense," Ted countered. "Once Forest Edge opens, we'll have children walking and cycling over the bridge to school."

Olivia considered it.

"It's not really a road safety issue though, is it?" she asked.

"Could be," said Ted. "Speeding cars, drunk drivers... a few of them have pranged a lamppost or gone into a ditch down the years."

"There was a fatality a while ago," said Tom. "A young woman called Alice – she was knocked off her bike."

"She came to a few of Charlie and Gloria's wine things back in the eighties," said Ted. "You might recall her, Sue."

Sue shook her head. "Sorry, no. I was hardly a regular visitor back then."

"I came to one when I was young," said Olivia. "I remember Gloria. I don't recall seeing Charlie though."

"No, well, they were probably apart at the time," said Ted.

"Right..."

"Alice was a sweet thing," said Tom. "She used to have pink streaks dyed into her hair – not something you saw very often in Maybrook."

That gave Olivia a jolt.

"Ancient history," said Ken, coming to join Ted and Tom at their table. "I'll take a wild guess and say you're discussing Steve Law's old campaign coming back to life."

"Spot on as usual, Ken," said Tom.

"Whether we need a new bridge or not has nothing to do with events of the last century."

"True," said Ted.

But Olivia was barely listening. Her memories of that first visit to Maybrook were vague. Gloria was little more than a thin face and a dress that made her look like a piece of summer sky floating around to cheer people up – although there hadn't been much cheer. She recalled wine with a terrible bouquet. Mum and Dad were there, bless them. And that had been the extent of her recollection.

Until now.

Somewhere on the very edge of memory… pink streaks.

"The accident was outside Gus's place, poor girl," said Tom. "Before Gus's time, mind."

That shocked Olivia.

But pink streaks. A fragment of memory long buried… it was there.

"Hello, we're Folkie-Karaoke," said Killy on the mic. "We're going to kick off with one of our most popular songs – 'Take Me Home Country Roads'…"

6

An Unusual Apartment

Just after half-five on Saturday, in welcome late afternoon sunshine, Bella was dragging Olivia along Colshot Lane bound for Gus's place.

"Hey, you're supposed to be worn-out from our walk so we look normal!"

They passed the house that sat between Whitman Farm and the main road with Olivia grateful that no one was outside waiting to capture it on video. Not that she saw much of the owners. The place had been empty during her first year in Kent, but it was now home to a couple who also had a place in London – where they seemed to spend most of their time.

At the top of Whitman Lane, they paused before crossing the main road. In the distance, a bright red open-top sports car came screeching around the bend from the High Street. It soon roared past doing at least sixty miles an hour – a good hundred yards before the '30' speed limit gave way to the '70' sign. Olivia glowered at the driver but guessed he wouldn't have had time to notice.

Alice came to mind…

Checking left and right too many times, she and Bella scurried across the road.

Approaching Gus's premises, Olivia checked her watch. His text said he'd packed up for the day at five and would grab a quick shower. He may have only locked up thirty minutes ago but, when closed, his garage looked like it had been abandoned for decades. Maybe it was the big, dark blue, wooden double doors and the lack of any bright plastic trimmings or strip lighting.

She paused on the corner of Frampton Lane, which ran down alongside the garage. How many times had Ken visited Milly Ramsey down there?

She refocused on the matter in hand.

Stepping onto Gus's forecourt, it struck her that the only new feature was the large 'M.O.T. Testing Station' sign she'd suggested he put up. In her view, binoculars had been required to read the old one from ten feet away. She told him it was important that everyone knew 'Gus Brody Autos' could issue a certificate that would keep their car legally on the road for twelve months. Gus had insisted that everyone *did* know, but Olivia's persistence won the day.

From the rooms above the garage, a radio suddenly blared as a metal window frame swung open. One of the Bee Gees' slower numbers, by the sound of it.

"Well done, Bella," Gus called down. "You tell her who's in charge."

"That's not funny," Olivia called back.

She led Bella round the back, past Gus's old Toyota, and up a flight of iron stairs.

Compared with most homes, Gus's apartment was a little unusual. It wasn't a regular living space – more a suite of three 1950s offices. The door at the top of the stairs even had an old metal plaque stating, 'Staff Only'.

Gus greeted her with a smile, a kiss, and a bit of fur-ruffling fuss for Bella.

"Tea? Coffee?"

"Coffee, please," said Olivia, savouring his fresh cologne.

The front door led directly into the waiting room or lounge, where Bella made straight for her cushion – a deformed corduroy beanbag that smelled of stale dog. Bella felt right at home there, which was Gus's intention.

Gus, meanwhile, pushed open a door to the right marked 'Staff Washroom' – which was now a tiny kitchen and, through a second door, an even tinier bathroom.

The door to Olivia's left was marked 'Manager's Office', which was now a sparsely furnished bedroom. Each element of the converted accommodation was small and cramped and smelled vaguely of cars, although the latter might have been her imagination.

She once asked Gus why he hadn't removed or at least painted over the plaques, but he said he didn't want to hide the history of the place. This was something she supposed she approved of. Whitman Farm's history had all but vanished by the time she and her cousins took over. It was an ongoing pleasure to uncover its story. Gus's apartment though…?

Not that he was flush with choices regarding where to live. The business wasn't making money. It was hardly an irretrievable disaster, but it was losing between five hundred and a thousand a month.

As the Bee Gees gave way to Celine Dion, Olivia made herself comfortable on the sofa, which had once been the back seat of a 1977 Ford saloon.

"Sorry about Luke," said Gus from the Staff

Washroom.

"It's no problem."

From what Olivia had learned, Luke's Aunt Beth had persuaded him to give his dad a go, just for a short break. Beth had a new man in her life, so it was hardly a coincidence. Maybe Luke didn't like being piggy in the middle. Choices were in short supply though. Grandparents on his mother's side, being in Broadstairs, were fifty miles away from his school. Likewise, Gus's parents, who lived in Folkestone, weren't much nearer – and Luke, like Olivia, barely knew them.

"So what have you and Bella been up to today?" asked Gus.

He was coming in with their hot drinks and a pack of cookies on a small wooden tray.

"Not much. We went over the bridge this morning. I still can't see why it needs to go. It's so lovely. Perfect, almost."

"*Almost* is right. I'll have a chance of getting work from Forest Edge and Ralston when the new bridge opens. You won't find many people arguing against sensible, balanced progress."

"I'm not against you getting more work. It's just a shame, that's all. No one's going to stop on the new bridge to watch the ducks. Not with cars whizzing by at fifty miles an hour."

"I'm sure there'll be a speed limit."

As always, he looked relaxed – as if he'd just returned from a few days at a health spa where they piped in Enya's Greatest Hits. Maybe replacing brake pads was a lost Zen art?

Olivia didn't feel quite so chilled. It wasn't lost on her that this very moment might be the one where she specifically asked Gus to move in with her.

In fact…

Yes, right now.

"Luke's a worry," he said. "All this messing about isn't like him. He's more the type who makes an appointment and sticks to it."

Olivia delayed her offer. Perhaps later.

"I was looking at these earlier," he said, taking a photo album from the sideboard.

He flicked through a few pages.

"May I?" she asked.

He'd occasionally shown her the album, but it wasn't something he got out on a regular basis.

Taking it from him, she leafed slowly through full-page printed snaps of Luke, 4, with a tennis racket that was too big for him; Luke, 6, playing with a Lego set; Luke, 11, with a certificate for Excellence in Literature…

"That was the only time I saw him at an awards thing at school," said Gus. "He's got a whole box of those."

"You didn't go again?"

"Trust me, it was complicated."

"It's a lovely photo. You're very lucky."

"It was one of those rare occasions where some higher power decided to give us the perfect day. Everything went right."

Olivia felt that familiar flash of Jamie's lost potential.

To have a photo album…

She placed the treasure trove on the table, took a chocolate cookie from the pack, and relaxed back into the sofa/car seat. Bella's eyes opened. Then her head rose off her beanbag.

Obligingly, Olivia broke off a piece cookie and threw it. Bella's jaws snapped expertly down on the treat.

"Clever dog," said Gus.

"So, what's on the agenda?" Olivia asked.

"Good question."

Gus leaned over the coffee table to kiss her.

"I've got crumbs on my lips," she complained unconvincingly.

"Would you care to step into the Manager's Office?"

"It's a bit early for a board meeting," she said.

Moments later, they were under the duvet, hungry for each other. Hands and mouths. Fingertips…

Soon, Olivia's breathing became shallow. A calm before a storm that had her seeing beyond the flaking yellowed ceiling to a sense of beyond. The imagined sky, perhaps. Or a future more ideal than the one on offer. Her man, yes, but without the absurdity of his cramped office-apartment…

She refocused. Wandering thoughts would lead her away, like that time in West Sussex, when driving to a coastal beauty spot, she was so deep in thoughts about mortgage options that she missed the turn-off and ended up outside a carpet warehouse on an industrial estate.

She concentrated. And those sensations began to gather again… she was one with her man… everything was perfect… and afterwards… she'd ask him to move in with her.

Focus, woman, focus…

And once more the sensations began to rise… until…

A knock!

She and Gus pulled apart and stared hard in the direction of the front door.

Rat-a-tat-tat!

In the lounge, Bella began growling from the safety of her cushion. Olivia guessed it was a territorial thing – risking life and limb to protect Whitman Farm, yes. Having to get off a cushion to protect Gus's place? Er…

Meanwhile, with a groan, Gus hauled himself out of

bed, pulled his clothes on and went to answer it.

Olivia soon heard two voices in the main room. It was Luke. He was a day early. Or a day late.

A moment later, having hastily dressed, she stood in the bedroom doorway, intent on a cheery hello, and hoping she hadn't put her jeans on back-to-front.

The young man was quick and knowing.

"Not interrupting anything, am I?"

7

Three's a Crowd

Luke was tall and thin with long, greasy swept back mousy hair, tired blue eyes, and a touch of acne. To add to this, he was wearing a sweaty white X-Men T-shirt over torn denim jeans and a pair of scruffy desert boots that appeared to have trekked twice around the world. His whole demeanour was weighed down by a battered red rucksack that had clearly journeyed even farther than the boots. He certainly looked much older than his last photo taken at fourteen. He was now fifteen going on twenty.

Olivia tried to think of something positive to say.

"Well, Luke, it's…" *terrible timing* "…a lovely surprise. We thought you were coming tomorrow for lunch."

"Change of plan."

"Hot or cold drink?" Gus asked.

"Same as you guys."

"Coffee then. Do you want another one, Liv?"

"No, this one's still warm," she said, eyeing the barely touched drink from earlier.

Gus withdrew to the kitchen.

"Your dog?" Luke asked.

"Yes, Bella."

"Bella…"

Luke made no move towards the dog, neither did Bella look ready to move off her cushion.

"So… how's school?" Olivia asked.

She tried not to cringe inwardly at such a lame question.

"School?" he replied. He pulled the rucksack off his shoulder and dumped it on the floor by the sofa. "At the moment, it's Literature. Drowning not waving kind of thing. Do you know Stevie Smith? I was much too far out all my life…"

Olivia tried to reconfigure how she might handle this too-confident young man. For that's what he was – too confident and not a boy at all. His voice was deep. He had stubble on his chin – not much of it, but…

"Literature? Lovely," she said, before wondering if to swap brains with Bella. "So, poetry, I'm guessing."

"Poetry, yes. They are not long, the days of wine and roses."

Olivia tried to process it but wasn't given time.

"Ernest Dowson, 'Vitae Summa Brevis'," he informed her as he took a seat.

"Right, well, *carpe diem* then," she said, not quite warming to Luke's reference to the fleeting nature of youth. "Seize the day."

"Yes, seize the day, from the Roman poet Horace. Enjoy life while you can. *Carpe diem quam minimum*… uhh… *credula postero.*"

Olivia smiled, or more properly grimaced.

Since learning of Luke's intention to visit, she had experienced a few fanciful moments where they grew together as a family at Whitman Farm. She chastised herself each time though. Becoming an instant family wasn't on the agenda. She didn't know Luke at all. She wasn't even sure which approach to take. Hold back? Step forward? The last thing he'd want would be for her to come across as some kind of mother-figure.

"So, back with Dad for the rest of the weekend?" she asked.

"Olivia…" said Luke, getting his phone out. "From Twelfth Night. Bang in the middle of all the comedy and romance. Of course, she has more than one suitor."

"Luke, don't tease," said Gus from the kitchen.

Luke smiled sweetly. "Olivia, from the Latin oliva – olive. It's okay, I'm not a Wiki on legs, I googled it on the way over. You grow grapes though."

"I do. Tell me about Twelfth Night. I didn't know I was in it."

"Hmm, well…" He checked something on his screen. Something of national importance by the look of it. Then he put the phone down on his knee. "It's about the twins Viola and Sebastian. They're separated in a shipwreck. Everyone falls in love. Lots of misunderstandings."

"I see…"

Luke eyed the kitchen door.

"Dad, I thought I might stay here for the summer holidays. Is that okay?"

There was a pause before Gus spoke.

"Yes, you're welcome to stay. You know that."

As far as Olivia could work out, it was the last thing Gus would have been expecting.

"It won't get in the way of anything?" Luke asked, still facing the kitchen.

"No, of course not."

The fifteen-year-old schoolboy turned to Olivia and smiled.

Olivia did her best to smile back.

"Well, that's all sorted," she said, feeling a little uncertain of the situation. Gus and Luke would be together for the six-week summer holidays. And it wouldn't get in the way of anything.

8

Wine Class

Just after six on Wednesday evening, the early June sun blazed from a clear blue sky over Kent. Summer was well under way.

Driving along an almost empty countryside highway to her class, Olivia embraced the feel of it all. This was her life. Grapes and wine. Not teenage boys.

She began singing 'Take Me Home Country Roads' – something the band had played in the pub the other night. It was the song she requested all that time ago at her first Folkie-Karaoke session. Or maybe it had been Annie who had suggested she request it? It didn't matter. The main thing was to belt it out right now at the top of her voice and only pause during those moments a car was coming the other way and she might be seen.

A short while later, she pulled into the car park of the ivy-clad Hallam Hotel. She was impressed. Set back from the road in extensive grounds, and with a portico entrance straight out of the 1850s, the imposing structure clearly had a history of horses and carriages and well-to-do visitors in far-off times.

She wondered – would people in the 22nd Century romanticize her arrival in a red VW Polo? Would they see that as charming and want to watch TV shows about people who drove around in small German cars?

Entering the hotel, she took in the relaxed atmosphere of a spacious lobby that was oddly monochrome. A style statement, no doubt. But she wasn't there for the décor. She was entering the world of wine – at Level Two. At least it wasn't Level One, which probably meant learning how to unscrew the cap.

Should she have booked a cab? No, she had zero intention of getting sloshed. This would be a professional engagement. Besides, having paid good money, it was important to remember everything.

Yes, this was serious. Eight evenings with a forty-minute multiple-choice exam rounding off the final session. She would have fun but study hard.

"Wine classes?" she asked a young man at the reception desk.

"The Cartwright Room, just through there," he said, pointing to the open doors of a function room where a few people had already gathered just inside the entrance.

"Thanks," said Olivia.

Her phoned pinged. It was text from Gus. 'Luke's here. He's staying overnight. See you tomorrow x'

Olivia let it wash over her. She'd been looking forward to supper with Gus and sharing news about her wine class. Luke turning up must have been a surprise. He'd left on Sunday evening without any inkling he'd be back so soon.

She thought of her final words. "You guys are going to have a wonderful time together this summer. Maybe we could squeeze in some three-handers?" Gus agreed and they both turned to Luke, who could have given the three-hander suggestion his approval but chose not to.

She pinged a short, supportive reply and made her way to the class.

Upon entering the airy Cartwright Room, a smart middle-aged woman greeted her.

"Hello, I'm Hannah Lincoln." She was standing by a mounted placard that declared: 'Wine Class, Level Two: 6:30 p.m.'

"Hello, I'm Olivia Holmes. I joined online."

Hannah studied a printed list and smiled.

"Lovely to have you along, Olivia. We'll be getting under way in a few minutes. If you could put your first name on one of those, so we know who's who."

She was indicating a table with blank yellow lanyards and black felt pens.

"Thanks," said Olivia.

She duly wrote her name on one and placed the ribbon around her neck.

While Hannah chatted with the next arrival, Olivia joined the others, who were making their own introductions. She was soon smiling at an elderly chap called Nomnar, which sounded like a character from Lord of the Rings. At least, that's what the spidery writing on his name badge seemed to say.

"I'm Norman," he said, which helped somewhat.

"Hello Norman, I'm Olivia," she replied, pointing to her own badge.

"I'm eighty-two," he added matter-of-factly.

Olivia beamed, but if he thought she'd be sharing her age, he could think again.

"I'm looking to learn everything about wine," Norman continued. He didn't seem to need much prompting. "I intend to build up a genuine understanding of the entire subject. That's why I'm happy to be on a beginners' course."

"No, it's Level Two, surely?" said Olivia. "*Advanced* beginners."

"Level Two, the beginners' course," he insisted. "I did Level One. That was just a taster – if you'll pardon my little joke."

Olivia grinned. Little? It was microscopic.

A few minutes later, they were ready to begin.

"Hello everyone," said tutor Hannah, addressing the dozen members of the class. "Welcome to the first of eight evenings on our summer Level Two course. It's always quite cosy, this one. We get all the best weather but smaller class sizes as some people won't commit to dates that might clash with summer getaways."

"I'm not going away," said Norman.

"Right, good… so, I see a few Level One survivors and some new faces. Welcome all. I'll get you to introduce yourselves in a moment, but first let me tell you a little more. Mainly, we'll delve into wine in more detail than we did at Level One. Level Two will give you enough knowledge to add a little professionalism for those in the sales and customer service side of hospitality, retail, and wholesale. It's also ideal if you simply wish to develop your knowledge of wine. By the end of the course, you'll understand wine tasting and evaluation, you'll be comfortable comparing and describing various wine styles, you'll understand wine labels, and you'll be able to give competent advice on selecting wines."

"And we'll taste more wines than we did at Level One?" asked Norman.

"Yes – and we'll taste more wines as per the brochure and course materials emailed to you, Norman. Now, over the eight weeks, we'll be taking on a number of learning objectives, but initially we'll focus on familiar grape varieties and wine types. We want you to have fun tasting and learning about wine. I'm also hoping I can inspire you to stay with us for our more advanced Level Three course which starts in October and runs on Tuesday evenings."

"I've already signed up for it," said Norman.

"Fantastic," said Hannah, her smile not wavering. "There's no rush, of course. Probably best to see how you get on here. Now, who'd like to say hello first?"

"That'll be me," said Norman. "I'm eighty-two and I've put away a few bottles in my time. The thing is, I've never really known what I'm drinking. I love red, but… well… that's my excuse for being interested in learning and tasting."

Olivia's own first experience of tasting came back to her. Sampling little bottles with Cass in North London. The details were vague, but she recalled her insightful appraisal of, "I'm getting red berries… red fruitiness… and red waftiness…" before singing, "Tiny little bottles, had quite-a-lottles."

They probably do things differently here…

Next to introduce themselves was a well-groomed, smartly dressed man of about her own age.

"Hello everyone, I'm Spencer and I love wine. On that basis, I thought I'd learn a little more."

He seemed friendly. She might have gone as far as fanciable had she not been serious with lovely Gus.

Next came a woman who was also around Olivia's age.

"Hiya, I'm Gail. I love wine and I'm planning to stay at a vineyard this summer. I've got my eye on France because I know someone who knows someone who just, might, possibly – fingers crossed – know someone. Just need to find the man of my dreams to go with me. Just kidding. Happy to go solo if need be. Anyway, I'm waffling. I signed up for this as it fits in perfectly. I wouldn't want to visit a vineyard without having *some* knowledge."

Visiting a French vineyard? Olivia warmed to the idea.

Next up was sixty-something Alicia, who bored everyone by having *the most perfect son* who had saved such a lot of tax that he was treating his dear mother to wine classes. It was important to know more about the lovely champagnes she enjoyed *on a regular basis.*

Twenty-two-year-old Felicity was next. Young, fun, and full of fizz.

"I've recently started working in hospitality and my boss thought it would be useful for me to get the basics under my belt."

"That's a sound approach," said Hannah. "We pride ourselves on helping those going into hospitality. Is your boss paying for the course?"

"No."

"Ah… well, think of it as a personal investment. You'll receive a certificate that's recognized in your industry."

Olivia restrained a growl. The course wasn't cheap for a lowly-paid new entrant into a lowly-paid industry.

Three others introduced themselves before it was Olivia's turn. By then, any idea of mentioning her co-ownership of a vineyard was strictly off the menu.

"Hello everyone, I'm Olivia. I moved to Kent from London about eighteen months ago and I have a real interest in wine. Over the past year I've begun to learn my way around the supermarket shelves, but I thought… well, a good friend of mine thought it was time I learned properly. This class already has a really lovely feel to it, so I can't wait to get started."

Once the introductions were done, Hannah got down to business with a PowerPoint presentation.

"Okay, so let me explain things in a little more detail.

First up, we'll be looking at wine types. That's still wines, sparkling wines, and fortified wines. And we'll break those down into wine styles – that's sweet white, full-bodied red, and so on."

Olivia soaked up the glorious kaleidoscope of bottles and full glasses on the screen. It wasn't as much fun as soaking up the actual wine, of course, which was currently contained in bottles on a table by the wall, with the whites in ice buckets.

"Grape varieties," Hannah continued. "We'll study wines made from the main white grapes. That's Sauvignon Blanc, Chardonnay, Riesling, Verdelho, Semillon, and Pinot Gris. And the main black grapes – which gives us Cabernet Sauvignon, Merlot, Pinot Noir, Syrah/Shiraz, Zinfandel, Malbec, Sangiovese, and Nebbiolo. Can everyone see okay?"

"Yes," was the response.

"Good, so… we'll look at some named whites – Chablis, Sauternes, Pinot Grigio, and Sancerre. And some named reds – Claret, Chateauneuf-du-Pape, Rioja, Beaujolais, and Chianti."

"Will we taste all those?" Norman enquired.

"Some of them. And don't worry about all these names. They're in the course materials PDF attached to the welcome email."

"Is the exam difficult?" Norman asked.

"Not really. If you follow the course closely, you'll be fine. It's a forty-minute multiple-choice with a pass mark of 70%. I'm sure you'll all earn your certificate… and perhaps toast your success with a perfectly-chosen champagne, Chablis or claret."

"I've got a bottle of claret at home," said Norman. "I don't dare drink it. It was only £1.75 from a market stall."

Olivia cringed. Britain's cheapest bottle of claret would

probably taste like vinegar strained through used cat litter.

But Norman wasn't finished.

"It was a present from my sister, Glenys."

The class gasped.

"How do you know she paid £1.75 at a market stall?" Gail asked.

"No, I paid £1.75 at a market stall and gave it to Glenys as a Christmas present."

There was a collective groan.

"She gave it back to me nine months later," Norman continued, "as an 80th birthday present."

Olivia forced a smile onto her face. She noticed Spencer beaming likewise, and for a brief moment it became a shared grin. This was her life now. Grapes and wine. And she would accept it whole, even if it included people like Nomnar.

"Moving on," said Hannah. "Who's ready to try our first wine?"

9

Fox on the Run

It was a warm Thursday morning, just before ten, and Olivia was among the vines carrying out a plant-by-plant inspection. One of her occasional paid workers was on the far side doing likewise. Pleasingly, the micro-clusters were beginning to show small individual flowers. Timing-wise, they were late compared with her first year – but then Nature didn't jot dates on a calendar.

Bella's role in all this involved flopping down under a vine, snoozing for a bit, and then, when Olivia had moved more than twenty feet away, getting up, trotting to her side and flopping down again, no doubt in the forlorn hope that she wouldn't have to keep repeating this exhausting process.

"Argh," Olivia gasped.

A fox stared back at her from under a vine.

Bella growled but held her ground.

"Hello, fox," said Olivia.

She was a little disturbed to watch it run off with a limp.

Her phone pinged – a text from Gus.

'Just a heads-up. Luke didn't go to school this morning. He says he's not well. Can we cancel lunch and dinner? Really sorry x'

She didn't see that she had much choice.

She typed: 'Yes, of course. Tomorrow then x.'

Gus replied, 'There's nothing wrong with him but I prefer to choose my battles. This won't be one of them.'

Olivia replied with 'xx' then tucked her phone away.

She wasn't sure what to do about Luke. She wasn't sure what to do about a limping fox either. It wasn't as if she could catch it and administer aid. In the countryside, there were farmers who would shoot it.

The fox disappeared into Charlie's nature reserve. Olivia and Bella followed.

Unsurprisingly, the fox broke through the practically non-existent boundary fence. It then darted to the right on Moorcroft's land, running along the boundary with Whitman Farm and, farther on, the boundary with Cam's brother's field. It would probably disappear somewhere by the rear of Alan Curtis-Fisher's place a few hundred yards away.

"Oh well, nothing we can do."

Her phone pinged again.

Gus…?

It was Vineyard Viv with a nudge to watch her latest video.

Olivia did so. A poem. A lovely one, too, about the beginning of summer. Viv seemed to radiate sunshine.

The one time they met, Viv said it would be fun to have a Viv and Liv episode for her YouTube channel. But Olivia was too self-conscious to act silly in a video. What if anyone she knew saw it?

They had chatted, of course – many times in the

YouTube comments section and via the occasional text. Olivia had come know that Viv was a happy single mother of a daughter. But doing a video with her…?

Olivia got back to studying her flowering vines. They were self-pollinating, of course. The caps on the buds would soon come off, pollen would be dropped, and the breeze would dust the pollen over the waiting stamens. The result would be tiny, healthy, bouncing, baby grape berries, unless, as Viv once said on YouTube, "one of the things that *can* go wrong *does* go wrong."

Fortunately, Viv had a dance to ward off evil anti-fertility spirits. Olivia smiled. It would be done again this year. Tomorrow, perhaps. But would she get in touch with Viv to arrange a meet-up in person?

*

Just before lunchtime, Olivia was preparing to take Bella for a walk when the doorbell rang. Bella reacted with her usual gusto.

"Hey, when Luke knocked at Gus's door you were too scared to move!"

On the doorstep, a beaming Steve Law handed over a box file.

"I had second thoughts," he said.

Olivia looked from the box to Steve, who had to be in his eighties. He seemed an earnest sort.

"Second thoughts about what?"

"Road safety. Thirty-odd years ago, I ran a campaign to have huge 'slow down' signs put up, the speed limit lowered, and bumps put in the road. It fizzled out, but I never throw away important documents. You never know when they'll come in handy."

"Right," said Olivia, feeling the weight of the box,

which wasn't much.

"I gathered everything I could to give the broadest possible appeal. It might give you a few ideas."

"Thanks, I'll take a look."

"Great. Let me have it back when you're done. I like to keep my records intact."

A thought occurred.

"Were you ever a council member, Steve?"

Steve pulled himself up to his fullest height, like a proud soldier on parade.

"Twelve years, three terms – mid-80s to the mid-90s."

"Well, thanks again."

A moment later, she placed the box file on the coffee table in the lounge. Bella looked ready for walking, but Olivia couldn't resist a quick peek. Inside were various letters to the district and county councils and to the local Member of Parliament. And there was Alice – Alice Osborne – looking back at her from the folded page of a local newspaper report which stated that the 50-year-old hit and run driver was caught, fined, and lost his license for five years.

Poor Alice…

She thought back, stretching her brain… at nine or ten years of age… didn't she decide to have pink streaks when she grew up? She never did, of course.

She looked up at Gloria's photo – the seaside bathing costume one. To come from being an office worker in London where she sat in the corner by the fire exit… to come from that to this. She sensed Gloria saying that tangling with the local elders would be taking on too much.

She wondered what Jamie would think.

Oh, you agree with Gloria, do you?

"Come on, Bella."

They were soon heading down Colshot Lane.

Reaching the point where it curved round to the left, Olivia paused. If Alan Curtis-Fisher had any real influence, there might soon be a new stretch of road opposite the bend, over on the right – a spur of fifty yards across common land to join the main road. The lane between here and home would be blocked off for cars. Yes, it would be quiet outside her front door. Outside Cam and Ken's too.

She continued round the bend, where Colshot Lane would be widened as far as Potter's Lane – but it was perfect here and she didn't want anyone spoiling it.

Reaching the right-hand turn that was Potter's Lane, she looked a little farther down Colshot Lane, a stretch that would remain untouched by progress.

Cam's brother, Tony's place was over on the left. He owned the five-acre multi-crop field behind Cam's small plot that adjoined the vineyard. With Tony having an eye on early retirement in a couple of years, it wasn't lost on Olivia how its potential might best be tapped.

She let Bella off the leash with a ton of praise and a treat.

"Now, let's get to the bridge in an orderly fashion, okay?"

Bella picked up a scent and headed off in a different direction, farther down Colshot Lane. Worried it might be the scent of the fox, Olivia followed in pursuit, crossing the lane and passing Tony's place before catching Bella at the gates to Alan Curtis-Fisher's estate.

Having secured her dog, she took in the scope of the parish council chairman's property for the first time. Its front ran alongside the lane for at least two hundred feet with the house towards the far end. It looked stylish with a curving gravel driveway leading over to the house.

The one thing that stood out for Olivia though was the notice stuck to a post by the entrance.

'Callers by appointment only.'

"Obviously, the fox wouldn't have dared come through here," she decided – although she peered down quiet Hopton Way, opposite the Curtis-Fisher estate, just in case.

"Come on, Bella."

They made it back to Potter's Lane safely. As far as she knew both sides of the lane were private fields and not for sale – at least not until the land was worth a lot more to the owners.

Bella was happy – having been freed once again from her leash to wander across the generous grass verges. That wouldn't be possible with fast-moving traffic on the new road. She couldn't believe Gus actually agreed with the proposed changes. Well, she could, of course.

A little way ahead, the bridge looked serene. Had she been a painter, she would have captured it in a dozen ways. Different seasons, different weather. It even occurred to her to try – although, given her lack of skill, she doubted anyone would appreciate its beauty on the canvas or even be able to work out what she'd painted.

Reaching the bridge, she paused to gaze into the water. It really was a special place. Or was she wrong about that? Was it just an ordinary place that stood out because she was still a newcomer?

She continued onward, over the bridge, and followed the curve of the road to the site of the new development. Here, a sign stated: 'Forest Edge, 120 new one-, two-, and three-bedroom homes.' Most would be for sale, with the remainder coming under a fair rent scheme.

The groundworks team that had started digging and levelling had stopped for a lunch break, leaving her free to inspect their work from the perimeter mesh fence. Concrete bases would soon provide the platform to start laying blocks and the whole development would quickly rise to dominate this part of the landscape. That was fine though. She wasn't in Kent to prevent people having somewhere to live.

Although…

She wondered if people centuries ago took against new developments. What she considered picture postcard villages – were they once the blight of the countryside?

She supposed not.

"Come on, Bella, you're tired enough to pass for a trained pooch. Let's hit the High Street."

10

Lunchtime

With the lunchtime sun almost overhead, Olivia and Bella strolled up to the main road in fine form. Owner and dog in perfect harmony. There was a little part of Olivia that wanted people to see them and note how well-behaved the dog was and how well the owner had trained her.

Passing the garage, she looked for Gus – but he was busy with a phone call, so she just waved.

"We'll say a quick hello on the way back," she told Bella.

As they reached the High Street, Ken and Beano were coming along. Ken was wearing a straw hat and had a newspaper tucked under his arm. It was too hot to stand there for long though, so Olivia decided to keep it short.

As they exchanged greetings, Ken slipped Bella a chewy treat.

"Steve Law popped some stuff round," said Olivia. "Documents that might help with a road safety campaign."

Ken's nose wrinkled.

"It'll be old stuff. You need to start afresh. It's a

different world these days."

"True," said Olivia, conceding the point.

"Are you sure you want to launch a campaign? You need a very clear focus for that sort of thing."

"Weirdly enough, I've never said I wanted to launch a campaign. People just seem to be good at advising other people to do things around here."

"You're not wrong."

Olivia was about to continue on her way, but thanks to Steve Law, Alice was there, on the edge of memory… with pink streaks in her hair.

"Do you remember anything about her? Alice, I mean."

Ken puffed out his cheeks.

"She was from another village. I'm not sure which one. It was just one of those things."

"Oh well…" said Olivia, letting it go.

She wished Ken and Beano well and walked on.

"Bella? Just do as Beano does, okay. It's that simple."

They got as far as Maybrook Newsagent's without incident. Then, as Olivia attempted to buy a crossword magazine, they encountered an interloper in the shape of a terrier-like dog. For some canine reason, it took an interest in sniffing Bella's rear end, taking the kind of care that Olivia was hoping to learn at wine classes.

"Go away," she told the dog.

There was no point in reporting the matter to its owner, a self-absorbed middle-aged woman who was busy arranging lunch on the phone, so she tried to gently nudge it away with her leg.

"Shoo, shoo," she urged without success.

Unexpectedly, the dog received a sudden, sharp yank on its chain.

"Come away, Chester."

"Lovely dog," said Olivia, smiling as best she could

while thinking Chester should be placed on some kind of offenders' register.

"Sorry about that," said Chester's owner. "I'm a new pet parent. On the way here, he barked at a man washing his van and started eating his sponge."

"Right…"

"And on Saturday, while we had my son's new girlfriend over for lunch, Chester was on the floor in front of them, wrestling with a pair of my husband's dirty underpants he'd stolen from the laundry basket."

"Ugh."

"Skidmarks and everything."

"Oh my."

"But dogs are amazing. They never judge us and they love being our best friend."

"Great."

"Ah, here's my mum – Eliza. She's big on training. Mum, meet a fellow pet parent."

Olivia smiled at a tall, thin, elderly woman with a face that radiated suspicion and distrust.

"Hello, I'm Olivia." She looked down to Bella and said, "Say hello to Eliza."

In dog-speak that meant sniff Eliza's crotch.

"I'm wondering if the previous owners bothered with training," said Olivia, pulling Bella away and pretending that nothing had happened.

"I think we know the answer to that," said Eliza. "Please do train your dog. If you have a small personality, make sure there are no distractions. Be ready with treats and games. Make sure there's nothing else on offer. Then, gradually, begin to get your dog to obey your commands. Sit. Lie down. Roll over."

Olivia fought the urge to comply.

A few minutes later, with her magazine in hand, she

headed for the Royal Standard's beer garden where Bella could drink from the steel water bowl by the side door.

Taking a seat, she let her dog off the leash so that she could slurp freely. As it was, Bella drank greedily for a few moments and then, continuing the greed theme, availed herself of a small baguette packed with bacon that, moments earlier, had been on the plate of a middle-aged man at a nearby table.

Olivia had seen him before, although on that occasion, his face hadn't been puce with rage.

Her phone rang. It was Sue.

"Fancy some lunch?"

"Great. I just have to buy some guy a sandwich first."

"I'm not interrupting anything, am I?"

"No, of course not. Why would you think that?"

*

Cam welcomed them at the front door. In a certain light, Olivia could see him as a bald Harrison Ford, hellbent on fighting evil Nazis, Galactic Empire stormtroopers, and weeds in his vegetable patch. Of course, driving instructor Cam's Nissan hatchback was hardly the Millennium Falcon...

He showed them through to the dining area in the newly completed rear extension, where Sue was setting the table.

Bella slurped some water from a bowl just outside the open patio doors and then flopped down to snooze.

"Someone's had a good walk," said Sue.

"I took her over the bridge," said Olivia, deciding to omit the Royal Standard bacon baguette incident.

"Ah, it's so peaceful down there," said Sue.

Cam said nothing. Being a driving instructor, his views

matched Gus's. A new bridge would mean easier access to potential learners at Forest Edge and Ralston.

Olivia took her seat and poured herself some orange juice.

"They've started work on the foundations at Forest Edge," she said. "It won't be long before it takes shape."

"It won't be long before they make a tidy profit then," said Cam. "They got that land cheap."

"Well, it's farther from the village," said Sue.

Cam shrugged. "Once it's up and running, you'll have more developments filling in the space to the bridge, and most likely on our side too in Potter's Lane."

"It'll be a lot busier," said Sue. "I wonder if Alan's idea might get any traction."

"Almost definitely," said Cam, clearly having been updated by Sue. "He may be full of bluster, but he's good at judging the public mood and understanding the likelihood of a project getting funding."

Olivia took a sip of juice then placed her glass back on the floral drinks mat. Ideally, they would retain the pedestrian and cycle route. Drivers could go north through Ralston and then east to join the main road. It would mean a three-mile loop to get to Maybrook when it was just over half a mile away, but…

But what?

Steve Law came to mind.

"You're a professional road user, Cam. Do you think there might be a road safety issue?"

Cam looked at Olivia as if she'd asked whether he might take up Sumo wrestling.

"I don't quite follow."

"I know the new bridge and widened roads might be good for business, but might they be less safe for cyclists?"

"They'll be no better or worse than other roads in the

area."

Olivia thought of a young woman with pink streaks in her hair.

"Do you recall an incident involving a young woman called Alice? It was a while back… it happened near Gus's garage."

Cam seemed surprised by the direction the conversation had taken.

"I do. It was a long time ago though. Thirty years or more. It's hardly supporting evidence for the case against the new bridge."

"No, I suppose not," said Olivia, backing off. "Mmm, the quiche looks lovely."

"Another of Sue's home-made recipes," said Cam with pride.

"I've had time since I retired," said Sue.

Olivia was well aware that baking had become a bit of a thing for her cousin.

"Just as well," said Cam. "Sue's agreed to support the village fete this summer by running a cake stall."

"*Helping* to run a cake stall," said Sue.

"Well, I'll certainly buy as many as I can," said Olivia.

Tucking into a generous lunch, they fell into an easy silence.

It was Cam who broke it a few minutes later.

"Alice…"

Olivia looked up.

"Yes, Alice – the young woman who…"

"Going back further, maybe forty-five years or more, she helped on the vineyard as a teenager for pocket money. I seem to recall she got on well with Gloria. Not everyone did. If my fading brain cells recall correctly, I think they were related."

Olivia was taken aback.

"Alice and Gloria?"

"Yes, Alice was something like Gloria's cousin's daughter."

"Well, it's nice to hear they got on," said Olivia, surprised that Cam's take on Alice didn't tally at all with Ken's.

11

Parenting Is Easy

The following morning, having left Bella at home on guard duty, Olivia was passing Gus's place on her way into the village. He was nowhere to be seen, so she assumed he would be upstairs with Luke, who was off school again. No doubt he'd be lounging around glued to his phone.

She decided to leave them to it.

In the High Street, that assertion changed. She spotted Luke coming out of the charity shop.

She waved and called out.

He ignored her.

Or more likely he hadn't seen or heard her – even though that required a wholly new interpretation of the phrase 'more likely'.

She crossed the street and followed him.

He stopped and checked his phone. She stopped and checked hers.

What exactly did she plan to say?

He walked on, she walked on.

Alan Curtis-Fisher stepped out of the wine store right by Luke.

Luke stopped. Olivia stopped.

Alan Curtis-Fisher gave them both a curious look. Olivia didn't care. All he could possibly see was a middle-aged woman stalking a teenage boy.

"Are you following me?" Luke asked her.

"Me? No."

"Is everything alright?" Alan Curtis-Fisher asked the pair of them.

"Everything's fine," said Olivia.

He stared at her a moment longer before walking off.

Luke did likewise – in the direction of Gus's place.

Olivia wondered why he would play such a stupid game. She'd expressed only support. Obviously, there wasn't a vacancy for a stepmother. Not that she wanted to be one. Maybe in a fantasy, but not in real life, which was where she tried to spend most of her time these days. She just wanted to be friends, but there didn't seem to be a way in for her.

Not wishing to cause a scene, she gave him time to get ahead before following. A few minutes later, reaching Gus Brody Autos, she came across the proprietor whistling a vaguely recognisable tune while looking over some paperwork, possibly related to the small Ford beside him.

"Is Luke okay?" she asked. "I saw him in the High Street."

"He's just gone upstairs to watch TV."

"Oh? While he's off school with nothing wrong with him? Shouldn't you have found him a job to do?"

Gus stared at her.

"Welcome to the world of parenting."

Olivia wasn't sure how she felt about that.

"I'm still wondering what made him want to spend the

summer here."

"He's my son."

Olivia backed off. Gus was one hundred percent correct.

"I'm just saying – it was a surprise. A nice one though. It'll be great."

"Thanks. I hope so. And I'm sure you and me…"

"Of course."

Olivia felt fine. She'd bide her time regarding being with Gus. Luke clearly wasn't fine, but it wasn't her place to interfere. Hopefully, a summer with his dad would straighten things out. But she wouldn't vanish into thin air. She'd be around, on hand, ready to guide a teenage boy if needed – however that might work.

"His mum must have had strong genes," she said. "He doesn't take after you at all."

"He's not my biological son."

"Ohhh sorry – you can always rely on me to put my foot in my mouth."

"Don't be daft." Gus put his paperwork down. "Luke was eighteen months old when I met Melanie."

Gus is a stepdad…

At that moment, she decided to double down on her determination to support them both. This was no time for lightweights.

"We were very different people," said Gus with some hesitation. "Sometimes that creates a kind of chemistry – but maybe not the kind that lasts. As you know, we split up when Luke was nine and… well, he lost her a few years later. As of now, I just want to be here for him in any way I can."

There was a moment of silence. Then Olivia took the lead.

"I'm here if you need help."

"Thanks."

It wasn't long before she had a first chance at trying for a second chance. Luke was standing by the rear door to Gus's garage.

"Hi," she said with a cheery smile.

"Dad says you used to build homes on parkland."

Thank you, Gus!

"I only *helped* that happen. I never actually did it myself."

"Same thing."

She supposed it probably was.

"Luke, do you like cakes?" she asked, going for a crowd-pleaser. "I could get some chocolate muffins?"

"Ah, the siren luring sailors to a rocky doom, only with muffins not song."

"There's no rocky doom involved."

"That's pretty much what those sailors thought in the Odyssey. But, as you say, chocolate muffins. Why not."

"Perfect," said Gus, picking up his paperwork. "Now, if you two don't mind, I've got work to do."

Luke strolled through the garage, past Olivia, and out to the front by the fuel pumps.

She followed him.

"I was hoping we could get on," she said.

"The older people get, the greater the distance between them and the big issues." He was looking along the main road out of the village. "Climate change would be the obvious example. Massively important, but older people just let it slip from their minds."

Olivia followed his gaze… beyond where Alice had departed all those years ago.

She refocused.

"Sorry, you were saying…?"

"Climate change."

"Yes, I'm very much interested in battling it."

"I thought Kent winegrowers would welcome warmer temperatures," he said, turning to face her.

"Well, there's not much I can do about that."

"You prove my point."

"Luke, the only difference I can make is living in the most responsible way I can."

"So where were your jeans made?"

"Pardon?"

But Luke lost interest.

It didn't matter though. She had time to get this right.

"I'll get those muffins," she said. "Shall we have them at my place?"

"No, here's fine. I have some reading to do."

Olivia smiled benevolently and wished him a good day. She then set off back to the High Street. The question was – how could she best deal with Luke without hiring a Mafia hitman?

No, this was serious. If she were to sneak into the world of parenting, she would need information.

She did a spot of googling on her phone as she walked and found a parental advice blogger. There was a video with a title that sounded about right: Building Parental Relationships.

She turned a few yards down Southway to be away from any prying eyes. A middle-aged woman appeared on her screen.

'Having trouble with a fellow human being who just happens to be your two- or three-year-old child?'

Ah, it's for toddlers. Still…

'Never forget, it's a relationship you're trying to build with a fellow human. If you remember that, they'll remember to visit you at weekends when they're forty.'

Olivia tried to picture a forty-year-old Luke on her sofa devouring a plate of chocolate muffins. Gus was yelling,

"More muffins, quick, or he'll never visit us again!"

'You love your child, right?'

For purely educational purposes… yes, I luvvy-wuvvy him.

'You love your child, but you're not getting good results.'

Correct.

'Whatever their age, whatever their stage of development, it's time to define your roles and impose some boundaries. Explain that parents have been making decisions forever. Explain how this applies all around the world.'

He's fifteen going on thirty – he'd quote Nietzsche at me.

'Is your child angry, frustrated, moody, sad?'

You forgot 'annoying'…

'We're talking about communication. Try taking a step back to see the context. A toddler could be teething. A teenager – maybe their boyfriend never returned their last few messages. If you can fix it, great. If not, then give them support. And if they don't want support, give them space.'

Blast him into orbit?

'Don't try to make your child happy 24/7 though. You'll both collapse with irritation and exhaustion. If they're older, you could share your own experiences at their age. If they see you're not an alien from another planet, they might feel you have the potential to be an adequate shoulder to lean on.'

Olivia put her phone away. She was now an expert in child psychology. That said, she was still going with the bribery approach.

Fifteen minutes later, she was back at Gus's with a paper bag containing three plump chocolate muffins.

But Luke wasn't interested in muffins.

"Speaking of food," he said to his dad. "Do you remember that day trip to Folkestone?"

"Not the hot dog incident?" said Gus from under the bonnet of the Ford.

Luke smiled while Gus erupted into laughter.

Once again, Olivia was the gooseberry, but she smiled along. She had no idea what was so funny, but she wanted to look comfortable while they wandered down Memory Lane.

"You don't want to know, Liv," said Gus. "Silly boyish humour."

"Luke? Silly?"

"No, me."

At that point, it distilled into a kind of clarity. Gus was the boyish one who enjoyed larking around and watching football. Luke wasn't like him at all. They really had nothing in common apart from the father-son bond that Gus had taken on.

Then again, what did she really know about parenting? Just how easy was it to maintain bonds with a teenager?

Something Cam said came back to her… about teenage Alice. It was certainly an idea.

"Luke… this summer. How about working with me at the vineyard? A bit of light work for decent pocket money?"

Yes, working side-by-side just like Gloria and Alice, they would become friends.

"Sounds good," said Gus.

Olivia was pleased. Handling Luke wasn't all that difficult after all.

"So, what do you think?" she asked.

"I won't be here," he said.

"Oh?"

"I'm going to Scotland."

"Scotland?" Olivia and Gus squawked in unison.

"Edinburgh," Luke added.

Olivia was out of her depth. Lost with no roadmap.

"Well, I'll come back this afternoon," she said. "With the muffins."

12

Good Old Viv, Good Old Ken

On the way home, Olivia looked something up on her phone. As suspected, the siren was also known as the temptress – an archetype, a woman of immense allure and desirability, but one who is actually an unprincipled, soulless individual using her intellectual and emotional gifts to lure men into her sphere of control.

Bloody cheek.

Still, Luke would be five hundred miles away in Scotland for six whole weeks. That wasn't bad compensation.

No, she didn't want to think like that. Teenagers had every right to be stroppy and awkward. It was just having their attitude crash into other people's lives that she disliked.

A text from Viv popped up.

'New vid!'

Olivia checked it out.

Bathed in bright sunshine, Viv was among her vines

dressed head-to-toe in white – as if she were auditioning for a washing powder commercial. Her happiness was infectious as she explained her intention to recite a short Ode to Nature. Then she began.

'Will magic ever show itself?
Will it ever abound?
Will it always be hidden,
Never to be found?'

Under the summer sky, Viv proceeded to water a healthy potted shrub and the video ended.

Olivia smiled. Good old Viv. She was undeniably nutty, but she was warm and genuine. And she only lived three or so miles away. There really was no excuse…

She texted her.

'Do a vid together? Soon?'

Reaching home, she enjoyed Bella's crazy welcome.

"Yes, I know, Bella. I've been away on a six-year trek around the globe, so your slobbering is not at all over the top."

Extricating herself from her dog, she kicked off her shoes, dumped her things on the kitchen table, put the kettle on, and popped up to the bathroom.

A few moments later, she returned to find a paper bag on the kitchen floor.

Uh-oh.

She went into the lounge, where her dog was hiding behind a chair with her ears down.

"Bella, do you have any information about my chocolate muffins? They're missing in action."

Bella tried to hide further behind the chair.

"Are you sure you don't know anything? Only you have crumbs on your chin."

Bella said nothing, leaving Olivia to put her shoes back on and head once more into the village for muffins. She'd try blueberry this time – they might be luckier.

*

An hour later, with blueberry muffins safely in the cupboard, Olivia was on the patio with Bella. The dog training website was open on her phone.

"Okay, Bella, let's go over a few things for the benefit of dogs with short memories. First up, positive reinforcement is a fun way to train. It's essentially rewarding you with treats and praise for good conduct. It also helps to build strong bonds between us because you'll know me as Lord of the Treats. So… sit."

Bella did so and received a treat.

"Stand."

Bella failed to move, so Olivia hauled her pet's back end off the ground and gave her another treat. It took a few goes but Bella began to understand what probably seemed a wholly pointless but very rewarding exercise.

"This next bit is for me."

She read the information. 'It's easier to get results in a quiet setting, before moving on to a more challenging one. Never take an untrained dog to the High Street!'

The doorbell rang.

A moment later, Olivia and Bella were greeting Ken and Beano.

Once she had extracted her youthful dog from her elderly friend, she set up tea in the lounge – all the while wondering what Ken really knew about Alice. She couldn't quite bring herself to raise it without giving it a little more thought though.

"Still glad you joined the wine class?" Ken asked once

they were seated comfortably.

"Oh definitely. I love it. Thanks for giving me a push."

"It was only a suggestion."

"We have a lovely bunch of students and Hannah the teacher is fab."

"That's good to hear. I wonder if you'll cover the great champagnes at some point. Or perhaps that's Level Three."

They both took a sip of their tea.

"What do you consider to be the great champagnes?" she asked.

"I'm no expert – more of a romantic. For me, the greatest are those bottles they found in that shipwreck."

"I must have missed that."

"In the Baltic, a while back, some lucky divers found a box of 200-year-old Champagne bottles, all in good condition."

"Wow."

"One of them was an 1841 Veuve Cliquot. It's not exactly cheap at the supermarket, but this one went for thirty-four thousand dollars at auction."

"Wow again. Would that be your ideal tipple?"

"No, I'd spend a bit more and go for the 1928 Krug. It was King George the Sixth's choice too, so I'm in good company."

"I'll order a couple of bottles for your birthday then."

"I'll look forward to it."

Olivia laughed.

Good old Ken.

They finished up their tea and took a stroll into the vineyard, where her friend seemed pleased with the crop's progress.

"The weather forecast says this sunshine won't hold," said Olivia. "Heavy rain on the way."

"Hmm, not so good for pollination," said Ken. "You've been through it before though."

"Indeed."

That first time was never far from her thoughts. She wasn't quite the wide-eyed newbie anymore, but she would never shrug off those memories of how it was. She clearly recalled Ken telling her not to over-worry about pumpkins and peas, and later, after fruit-setting, that she should pick off the smallest bunches to improve the quality of the remaining grapes. She supposed she would always hear his voice when she was out among the vines.

"Dusty Miller's looking good," he said.

He was looking over the pinot Meunier, with its flour-dusted leaf undersides.

"It's *all* looking good," he added.

"Thanks, Ken. Let's hope for a good summer."

"So, how's your young man?" he asked.

"Luke? He's fine."

"A difficult age. His whole life is being shaped right now."

She thought of her offer, for him to work with her… and that triggered another thought – of teenage Alice working there all those years ago.

"He said adults aren't interested in important things like climate change. But we are, aren't we?"

"Do you care about those things?"

"Yes, of course."

"Me too, but there's not much I can do. I already use very little power and I walk everywhere."

"Luke's right to care, of course. Maybe I should get him interested in a less ambitious target. Something local…"

"This wouldn't be the bridge, by any chance?"

"Possibly – although I doubt I can save it – with or without Luke's help. Apart from Katy and her dad, I don't have any influence."

"No, but you might soon have a chance to change all that."

"How?"

"Have you ever thought of joining the parish council?"

"You're not serious?"

"It's not a matter of whether I'm serious. It's a matter of whether you're serious. They're going to announce a vacancy. It's mid-term so they'll try to fill it by co-opting someone."

"I can't see them co-opting me."

"No, perhaps not. I'm sure they have someone in mind. Changing the subject, tell me more about your wine classes."

"Changing the subject right back, what if I were serious?"

"If more than one person wishes to join the council, there'll be an election."

"I can't take part in an election."

"Exactly. So, tell me about wine regions. How does Kent shape up against the more established parts of the world?"

"I live and work here, don't I?"

"Yes…"

"Don't I qualify?"

"For what?"

"To stand in an election."

"Yes, you qualify."

"I wouldn't have the cheek to do it though."

Olivia imagined being a parish councillor – and just as quickly dismissed it. She'd only been in Maybrook five minutes. Well, eighteen months – but in a village, that was the blink of an eye.

"They wouldn't want me," she decided.

"Who wouldn't want you?"

"Old Roper, for one."

"You don't want to take any notice of Old Roper. He'll never join the parish council. He doesn't like taking responsibility. He just likes having his say."

A thought occurred. "Is there a Young Roper?"

"Yes, his son. But he did something shocking and terrible, so he's never mentioned in public."

Olivia was wide-eyed.

"What did he do?"

"He moved to London."

Olivia laughed, but the jollity quickly faded.

"Oh, I don't know…"

"I should point out you'll need ten backers if you decide to fight an election."

Olivia let the idea drop.

"No, it's a red herring. I'm not interested in local politics. As for the bridge, I'll email someone. I won't come to anything, but I'll feel better."

"You know best," said Ken.

"On this occasion, I do. My aim is to become part of the wider community, not to make a fool of myself."

13

Abra-ca-wotsit

That afternoon, under a heavy charcoal sky, Olivia approached Gus's place with a bag of muffins and the hope that some progress might be made. She was by no means an impatient person, but she was keen to get some positive vibes going as soon as possible. She didn't want Luke going back to his Aunt Beth without them being friends.

"Just finishing up," said Gus as she came into the garage. He was doing something with the headlights of an old Vauxhall.

"Is Luke upstairs?" she asked.

"Yes, he's reading. I say 'reading' because I made it clear that watching TV wasn't an option."

Olivia was glad to hear it.

"Is he okay though? I mean he'll be going back to his aunt's soon…"

"No, there's been another change of plan – he's staying on here for a week or two."

"Ah…" *Arghhh.* "That's great."

"I know he keeps messing about, but hopefully things will settle down. The Scotland thing's with a schoolfriend. They'll stay with the friend's cousin's family in Edinburgh and go to comedy shows at the Festival – that kind of thing."

"Good. I'm glad it's going okay. It can't be easy being a dad under these circumstances."

"I don't suppose it's the easiest job in the world under most circumstances. I bet even you caused your dad a few worries."

"Me?"

"Oh… look, sorry. I didn't mean to bring up…"

"It's okay."

Gus knew about her father taking his own life when his business failed. It wasn't something she wanted boxed away never to be mentioned. It was just that it would crop up at unexpected moments and catch her out.

Gus came and gave her a hug, which she appreciated.

"Not interrupting anything?" said Luke at the back door.

"No," said Olivia as she and Gus pulled apart. "It's you I came to see – bearing muffins, of course."

"Not sure if I fancy a chocolate muffin. Blueberry would have been good."

Oh really…!

Olivia raised the paper bag, gave it a quick shake, and tried to adopt a generally theatrical disposition.

"Abra-ca-wotsit!" She placed the bag on the car bonnet and tore it open. "Blueberry muffins!"

Luke seemed genuinely surprised.

"How…?"

"Sorry, it's a trade secret."

"Yes, well, while you're here, how about signing a petition. It's to save bees from pesticides. I can text you the link."

Gus tutted. "Yesterday, it was a petition to ban vinyl records."

While Gus went through to the tiny adjacent washroom and kitchenette to clean up and make the tea, Olivia swapped phone numbers with Luke to get his text, which felt like progress. She also seized the chance to engage further.

"Looks like Dad's busy today," she said.

Luke shrugged. "Yeah."

"Luke, about your dad and me…"

"It's okay, I *am* fifteen. Technically closer to sixteen. So, you and Dad…?"

"We see each other."

At least we used to.

"What do you get up to?"

"We talk, we walk, we watch TV. Sometimes we have a Chinese takeaway night."

A romantic Chinese takeaway night…

"Good," said Luke. "I love Chinese."

Great.

A wasp buzzed Luke. Olivia had some sympathy with the insect but helped him swat it away.

Luke was relieved at seeing it fly off.

"Useless, pointless… I hate wasps."

"Save the bee but not the wasp? I'm no expert, but Whitman Farm might struggle to get a decent bottle of wine without them."

"That's fake news. Wasps are born angry and love to sting people."

"It does seem like that, but Ken told me a fungus grows on grapes over the course of the summer… not sure of the name. It might be Saccharomyces cerevisiae – but anyway, it's a type of yeast, and because it's there right at the start, long before the winemaker gets involved, the wine tastes better."

Luke softened. "Go on."

"The yeast grows each summer and dies each winter. And I can see you've already worked it out. Wasps bite into the grapes and feed the mush to their larvae. Believe it or not, the yeast survives in their stomachs."

"And they carry it back to the vineyard?"

"Yes, the following year."

"The cycle of life, eh?" said Luke. "They'll still get swatted if they come near me."

"Fair enough."

She was looking for a way to find common ground, but there wasn't much to work with. Jamie's teenage trials and tribulations were limited, pretty much, to her own experiences. But Luke? Somehow, she suspected a less confident individual than the one he portrayed – as if he were using his intellect and knowledge to build a shield.

"Busy on social media?" she asked.

She was aware she sounded a century out of date.

"Social media? Yes, busy."

He went out to the front.

She supposed she only understood social media from an adult point of view. Teenagers had never been equipped to make continuously good decisions, but now mistakes could be shared with dozens, if not hundreds. Or worse, if it were utterly humiliating, it could go viral and be seen and laughed over by potentially millions.

Common ground…

She followed him outside.

"The bridge should be replaced soon," she said. "You know the one I mean? At the end of Potter's Lane."

"I know the one. Embarrassingly enough, I've played Pooh-sticks there. Not recently, I should add."

"Don't knock Winnie the Pooh. I'm a fan."

"Whatever."

"I'm in a minority but I think it's worth saving. I'm not against the new development, but cars should use the road north to get to the village."

"Dad says that means driving a long way round... and possibly not using his garage because they'll be over halfway to the next one."

"The bridge is one of the village's best attractions."

Luke shrugged. "It's not exactly *in* the village."

"By the time all those new developments are built, it will be. Anyway, it's a thing of beauty."

"True..."

But he didn't seem overwhelmed by her devotion to it.

"In fact," she said, reaching for a faintly unlikely scenario, "I plan to paint it."

"What? Graffiti?"

"No, I'm going to capture it on canvas."

"And do you have that ability?"

Cheek.

"It might not be around for much longer. Don't you think it's worth preserving?"

"Maybe."

"You're interested. That's good."

"Dad says you think it should be kept for walkers and cyclists."

"Yes."

He nodded a little.

I do believe we're getting somewhere.

"But you're not going to do anything about it," he added. "Not really."

Ouch.

"I'll do what I can, Luke."

"Such as?"

"Well…" *I need a really big fib about now.* "I'm thinking of campaigning to save it."

Luke raised an eyebrow.

"Thinking or doing?"

"Well… doing, obviously."

This would be it. She and Luke would join forces to save the bridge. They would fail, but they would bond thanks to their heroic joint effort.

"Do you like quizzes?" he asked.

Even better.

"Yes, I do."

"I've got a thing." He found what he was looking for on his phone. "Okay, so, you have to answer these questions to build a psychometric score."

Olivia frowned. "I was thinking of a music quiz or something."

"In ten seconds, name things you love."

"Love? Have we started?"

"Yes."

"Okay… Nature. The countryside. Um… freedom?"

Ugh, stupid…

"And now name things you hate."

Easy.

"Unfairness, bullying, miserable people…" *teenagers…* "the fact that there are so many calories in—"

"And now name things you fear."

"Will you be taking a turn?"

"Five seconds left. Answer honestly."

Loneliness…?

Gus arrived with their teas on a tray.

"It's not that daft quiz thing, is it?" he asked.

"Just because you scored low, Dad."

"Everybody scores low. That's what you wanted when you developed it."

Olivia was surprised.

"You created it?"

"It's just a basic app. A five-year-old could have built it."

Olivia puffed out her cheeks.

"Right… well… blueberry muffin, anyone?"

"Not for me," said Luke.

Why, you little…

"Thanks," said Gus, taking one.

"Olivia's going to save the bridge," said Luke. "Or so she says."

"You obviously don't know Liv," said Gus. "When she says she's going to do something, she gives it a hundred percent. She's not a lightweight."

Luke shrugged, but Gus wasn't having it.

"Your attitude at school, to exams, to your future… if you had a tenth of what Liv has, you'd smash it out of the park. You could do a lot worse than see her as a role model."

Olivia wondered if she should step in and tell Gus that she wasn't exactly superglued to the idea of spending months fighting to save a bridge.

"Commitment," said Gus. "It's what Liv has above and beyond most people I've ever met. She's the real deal and it's time you started respecting her."

Luke looked suitably contrite.

"I'm sorry, Olivia. I wasn't suggesting you were a lightweight."

"Good," said Gus, his gaze fixed on his son. "Now eat your muffin. Liv bought it specially for you and used magic to turn it from chocolate to blueberry."

14

Save the Bridge... Now!

On a bright Saturday morning, Olivia was among the vines checking for damage after rain. All seemed well enough, but pollination was upon them and having rain wash the pollen off the plants would always have the potential for unwelcome consequences.

Apart from that, council member Katy Law had been in touch. She had emailed a few key people at the district council and the developer's office. She was confident that the bridge was safe for now, although replacing it was still the plan. Nothing had changed. It was merely a stay of execution while certain avenues of interest were explored.

Olivia, of course, was committed to saving it. At least that's what Gus had told his son. Backing out would confirm her as a lightweight and give Luke a welcome excuse to backslide. That said, he'd only be around for a week or two more and then he'd be back with Beth for a month and then off to Scotland.

"Fancy a walk, Bella?"

Two minutes later, they stopped outside Ken's place. At least, Bella stopped, and Olivia had little choice but to stop too. Ken was at the window, waving, and came out to make a fuss of Bella and slip her a treat.

"Methinks a pattern is emerging," said Olivia, eyeing her pet with suspicion.

"It's no trouble at all," said Ken, although Beano looked miffed at his treats being handed out willy-nilly.

Shortly after, on the corner of Colshot Lane and Potter's Lane, Olivia was studying a large temporary sign fixed to a wooden stake.

'Bridge Ahead Closed To Pedestrians and Cyclists.'

She let Bella off the leash with a ton of praise and a treat.

"Now, I want you to stay. Okay? Stay."

Was that it? Did dog training culminate in a eureka moment?

Bella ran off towards the bridge.

Perhaps not.

At the bridge, all was well. Despite the new sign, it was still accessible to pedestrians and cyclists – meaning Olivia could stand on it and enjoy watching her dog ferreting by the water's edge below. But not for long. The lure of activity by the Forest Edge development was too much for Olivia to ignore.

Arriving at the site with Bella on the leash, she had her eye on a middle-aged man in a lightweight charcoal suit and yellow hard hat. All around, muddy diggers and people wearing hi-viz were making a noise. Bella didn't look at all happy.

Olivia took it all in. This was happening right now and Forest Edge would soon dominate the landscape hereabouts.

Luke believed adults weren't interested in big issues like

climate change. He was wrong. She *was* interested. But he needed a dose of realism. She couldn't save the world. She didn't have time. Small things though…

"Hi," she said to the man in the suit and hard hat. "I live locally and thought I'd take a look. Are you the surveyor?"

"Yes – it's all going well, as you can see."

Olivia chatted with him and learned a little about the timelines they were working to. A few months from now, the site would be unrecognisable.

It was as she was mentioning Katy Law that she noticed something odd. Despite the curve of the road between Forest Edge and the bridge, she could see across the open expanse…

"What the f—"

Olivia and Bella ran the distance in record time – at least record time for the human half of the duo, who arrived holding up a hand but unable to speak. The three-man wrecking crew stared at her in a way that suggested she wasn't being taken seriously.

"You… have to stop."

"Stop?" said the guy driving the digger. "We haven't started."

Looking very much the unhelpful type under a well-worn yellow hard hat, he revved up his cacophonous machine.

Olivia pulled her phone out.

"I have an email."

"Me too," said another wrecker, this one wearing a spotless white hard hat. "25% off if I buy six bottles of wine."

"This one's from Katy Law… parish council member. It's about the bridge."

"Parish council," said the driver. "I thought they went

out with Queen Victoria."

"They *came in* with Queen Victoria, but that's not the point. Katy says, 'have had feedback from Giles Smith stating that the District Council will take a look.'"

"We don't know anything about that," said the white hat. "Would you and your pet mind moving."

"We have a schedule," said the driver.

"A Saturday schedule," said the third man. "We'd like to finish early."

In shock, Olivia found herself and Bella stepping between the digger and the bridge.

"I'm a reasonable person," she said. "Please call your boss. They should have a message from Giles."

The white hat signalled to the driver, who switched off the engine. He then pulled out a phone and made a call.

"Is Danny there? It's Steve at Forest Edge… oh… okay, no worries. Ask him to call me back."

He ended the call and eyed Olivia.

"He left early. Golf, I think."

"Right, so… you'll withdraw then?"

"It's Danny, our boss. He might not get back to us until next week."

Olivia didn't trust them.

"I'm calling Katy."

"The one on the pretend council?"

"Parish council – yes."

Olivia did so – and got Katy's voicemail.

Great.

"Can we get on?" the white hat said.

"No, I'll wait here till Monday if I have to."

But I won't be outnumbered.

She called Gus. He took a while to answer.

"Gus, I could do with some help."

"Car or house?"

"Bridge."

"Pardon?"

She explained the situation, but Gus seemed to think she was exaggerating.

"I can't come, Liv. I've got a customer waiting."

"I wouldn't ask if it wasn't important," she said.

"I can't – sorry. Will Luke do?"

"Luke…? Yes, he'll have to do."

"Wait one sec. Luke! Luke…! Could you come down?"

There was a delay of three hours, or at least it seemed like it. Then she heard Gus speaking to him.

"Liv needs your help."

There was a faint mumble.

"It sounds like an emergency," said Gus.

Mumble-mumble.

"The old bridge in Potter's Lane."

Mumble-mumble.

"How should I know? Maybe she's fallen in."

The digger driver lit a cigarette while Olivia strained to hear a lengthy muffled discussion.

Finally, Gus came back to her.

"He's coming."

"Great."

"Thirty minutes."

"Thirty? He could run it in five!"

"Just try to stay afloat and watch out for sharks."

Olivia sighed. She had only known Luke a week, but her opinion of his reliability was already fully formed.

15

Photos and Paintings

On Tuesday, after a short, sweaty day in the vineyard, Olivia was finished and showered by three p.m., and in the lounge going through Gloria's box of photos. Down to the final few, there were some faces she couldn't identify. Family, possibly. She reflected on that – on family, on belonging.

She hadn't seen Gus the evening before. He'd phoned and apologised about Luke's attitude. That meant an evening with Bella, which had been fun, if less romantic.

But belonging…

Raglington Hall came back to her – the venue of her final Prior Grove team building weekend. She recalled oil paintings of various Raglington family members. Wouldn't it be something special to display the entire history of Whitman Farm with similar pride – albeit on a smaller budget?

And what about Alice? Did she belong, even in a small way?

Olivia went across the hall to the spare front room. This had a bay window identical to the one in the lounge, which was the only thing in the room to have received a lick of paint. She quite fancied a spot of decorating this summer. This room would have a pastel shade with a few framed photos on one of the walls. Family photos? Perhaps. She'd also blag a few pieces of furniture from Ed the house clearance man.

She glanced out at Colshot Lane.

A car whizzed by bound for the main road.

Then the doorbell rang.

Olivia and Bella answered it to find Katy Law beaming at them. Once Bella had been bribed with a treat, Katy was able to explain herself.

"I'm just walking round to see Alan. I thought I'd stop by to say the bridge is double-sorted this time. Everyone now knows it's to stay untouched until a final decision is taken."

"That's great, thanks. To think all that history was about to become rubble."

"History isn't always a priority. I think, in this case, the decision to go for a new bridge has only been delayed."

"I know. It's a shame though. Are you a fan of local history?"

"I love it, although my main thing is family history. I'm learning about my lot back in Victorian times."

"Sounds interesting."

"It is. It's taken a while, but I've found some brilliant bits and pieces: old documents, photos, lots of stuff online. Anyway, I ought to dash. Alan's expecting me."

Olivia waved Katy off then turned to Bella.

"I'm just going out for a while. Be good."

She gave Bella a bit of fuss and then headed off to the High Street.

On the way, she passed Gus's place. He was cleaning the front, which meant he had no work on.

She popped over to say hello.

"We're like a couple of teenagers," she said a moment later in his embrace, just inside the garage, out of sight of passers-by.

"Don't mention teenagers to me," he said. "We both know one who's been messing around at school again."

Olivia frowned.

"I'm sorry to hear that."

"I'll have to get going in a minute. I don't want to be late picking him up."

She kissed him and left him to clean up in time for the afternoon school run.

Outside, a mother and her toddler were passing by, chatting happily like a million other parents and their child did every day.

Olivia smiled at them. In the months and years after she lost Jamie, seeing such a thing would stir up strong emotions. Emotions that would have to be shut down. Time had, of course, calmed such reactions, but having Luke around had stirred something. Not as powerful. That could never be. But undeniably *something*.

She wanted to be involved. She wasn't sure how, but she would engage with him. Maybe not save the world together, or even save the bridge, but something that would involve Luke, even if it could only be via text and email. Somehow, that boy was going to have to accept that she and his father had a future together, which meant she and Luke needed to start seeing each other as friends.

She wondered if to take an interest in teen stuff. Virtual reality was a big thing now, wasn't it? She tried to see herself in plastic headgear, firing laser beams at Godzilla.

Maybe not.

*

Bathed in warm, late afternoon sunshine, Olivia was perched on an uncomfortable camping seat in front of a canvas and easel – all borrowed from Cam, who she had discovered occasionally liked to paint.

Her brush was poised, a blue drip about to fall from it. An instant later, the drip formed part of the sky on a landscape she had tentatively called 'Bridge'.

By the time she got to adding the actual bridge, Ken had ambled along with Beano – both of them looking perky despite their years.

"Hiya Ken. Beano looks bright. Is he on double rations of those conditioning pills?"

"Yep – he's been banned from the Olympics twice now."

Ken came up to the painting and took a good look.

"That's not bad," he said.

"Thanks. I expect the Louvre will be on the phone before the day's out."

"Dog training seems to be working."

He patted Bella, who was sitting but leaning heavily against his leg.

"Slowly does it but we're getting there."

"Well, let's be honest, Beano was a yob when he was a pup."

"Really?"

"There were three cows in a field one time, and he tried to round them up."

"Did he manage it?"

"No, one of them mooed at him. Scared the life out of him, it did. He scuttled away, skidded through a juicy cow pat and leapt straight into my arms."

"So, there's hope," said Olivia, eyeing Beano with suspicion.

"There's always hope," said Ken.

Olivia smiled. But it wasn't dogs on her mind.

Ken looked at her painting again.

"Does it need people in it? Maybe people going somewhere? Like Lowry? Or fishing, like Turner?"

"Good thinking."

"Or maybe a family. Kids."

Too personal.

"Or a cyclist?"

"Great idea, Ken."

He laughed. "I practically lived on a bike when I first came to Kent. A right old bits and pieces thing it was. I went everywhere on it. There's something about being young and carefree…"

Olivia thought of Luke. And Alice.

"Ken… Cam said Alice helped at the vineyard as a teenager. He reckons she got on well with Gloria."

"That must be true then."

"You said she was from another village, but you didn't know much about her."

"It was a long time ago. Just one of those dreadful things."

She wanted to challenge him, but he was ninety. What did it matter?

But she couldn't just drop the matter.

"Cam said she was Gloria's cousin's daughter."

Ken said nothing, so Olivia continued.

"Three of us inherited her estate. Who knows, Gloria might have made it four."

"We've touched on fortune before," he said. "It's a fickle thing. Count your blessings and get on with your life – that's my philosophy."

He and Beano turned for home and Olivia got back to her painting.

But she was thinking of Alice.

16

Wine Matters

Early on Wednesday evening, Olivia pulled into a parking space at the Hallam Hotel and headed for her class. It was her second Wednesday and the prospect of spending two hours with fellow wine enthusiasts filled her with joy.

It had in fact been quite a wine day. Earlier, she and Sue had popped over to Ramsey's winery to see how their first year's produce was coming along. Archie, the winemaker from Canterbury delivered an encouraging update. They could have the first of their sparkling wine nine months from harvest – just in time for Sue and Cam's wedding. The bulk of their wine would be given an extra six to nine months.

Olivia could already see herself in the supermarket admiring Whitman Farm's wine on the shelves…

Once the classroom greetings were over, Hannah put Olivia with Gail and Spencer as one of four teams. Together, they would learn, taste, and combine notes. Then the teams would see how they varied in their assertions. Olivia was delighted. She really liked Gail, and Spencer was… nice.

"Hannah's a great teacher isn't she," she declared.

"Wonderful enthusiasm and patience," said Spencer, eyeing Hannah as she helped another group with their questions. "She also teaches in East Sussex."

Gail raised an eyebrow. "How do you know?"

"She told me."

Olivia smiled.

This guy's not shy.

"I expect they have to teach all over the place to make a living," she said.

"Deffo," said Spencer. "And you need to put yourself about more at Levels One and Two."

"Why's that?" said Gail.

"Terry takes the Level Three classes. They're longer runs so he only starts afresh twice a year. Hannah has to run four classes a year to get a similar number of paid evenings."

"Seems unfair," said Gail. "Couldn't they share?"

"Terry's been doing it twelve years; Hannah, three."

"Ah."

Spencer wasn't finished. "Yvette takes the Level Four students. That takes two years to complete."

"And how much experience does she have?" asked Gail.

"Thirty years."

"You sound like you'd like to do the whole package."

"I do. Don't you?"

"Possibly."

He turned to Olivia.

"And you? Might you go all the way?"

Olivia felt warm.

"I haven't decided."

"Wine tasting isn't as easy as people might think," said Gail.

"No," said Spencer. "What's the worst wine you've tasted?"

Gail laughed.

"Don't… a friend bought me a bottle of cheap pink stuff. Yuck."

"I'm sure we've all had bad wine," said Olivia.

"Okay then – the most interesting wine."

Olivia knew right away.

"It was last summer at a winery called Ramsey's. They wanted opinions about the potential sugar balance for a sparkling rosé."

"Oh," said Spencer, "so way before it hits the stores?"

"No offence," said Gail, "but why ask you?"

"No offence taken. The winemaker's opinion was the main one. They just like thoughts from all sides, that's all. I think I was viewed as a typical supermarket consumer, to be honest."

"Thing is," said Hannah, interrupting, "that's actually an important opinion. Do tell more. It's a part of wine tasting that many don't get to experience."

Everyone gathered around their new teacher.

"Well…" said Olivia, gathering her thoughts, "as I recall… we were presented with various bottles that were labelled with their sugar dosage. So, it was really about seeing how they were maturing. Our hosts popped half a dozen corks and we watched the wine fizz and foam. It probably sounds silly, but I was really excited."

"It's not silly at all," said Hannah.

"Well… the first one I tried was called… wait for it… very sexy stuff, this… Bottle 3."

"Bottle 3?" quizzed Norman.

"Along with dates and details, yes. The thing is, our

expert, Archie, made the point that we shouldn't try to think like experts. He just wanted our reaction. Basically, was this the sort of thing we'd happily pay good money for."

"Bottle 3…" Norman repeated.

"Yes, I expect it's called something else now. Basically, it had enough sugar to bring the best out of the grapes while staying in the dry range. Balance is everything."

"And that's it?" said Norman.

"Well, we looked for a good collar around the glass and a steady bubble train rising up through the wine. And small bubbles, of course. Then there was the bouquet…"

"And *that's* it?" said Norman.

"No… one other thing. We had to taste it at room temperature."

The class groaned as one.

"Well, no… if the wine is too cold, it masks the true extent of the sugar taste. Don't worry – the next day we went back to try them all again from the fridge. It's probably in wine stores all over the country by now."

"Bravo," said Hannah. "Really interesting stuff. I recommend anyone who gets the chance, takes it."

As they reformed into their groups, Gail had a question for Olivia.

"Do you dream of wine? Not wine, obviously, but, you know… the wine thing. The whole thing?"

"Um…?"

"You know… the dream. Living it. Wine. Grapes. Vineyards…"

"Well, actually… I do part-own a small vineyard."

Gail gasped.

Even cool Spencer raised an eyebrow.

"Oh my God," said Gail. "Olivia's doing it, actually living the dream!"

"Er… yes. It's not a dream, as such. More hard work. But I know what you mean. There are some days when—"

"I would *love* to live on a vineyard!" said Gail. "It must be like…"

"A dream?" Olivia guessed.

"Listen everyone," cried Gail. "Olivia owns a vineyard!"

What happened next hadn't been in Olivia's plans. She smiled apologetically at Hannah as once again everyone gathered around.

"Is it in France?" asked Gail.

"How big is it?" asked Alicia.

"Why are you taking a beginners' wine class?" asked Norman.

"Okay, let's get started," said Hannah. "I want to talk about Terroir and the Appellation system, but first let's go back to the Middle Ages, where Benedictine monks in Burgundy realized that different microclimates and soil conditions, coupled with a variety of winemaking techniques, created distinctive wines. This is where the French idea of terroir comes from…"

"I'd love to visit," Spencer whispered in Olivia's ear. "Is that possible?"

*

Returning home from her class, Olivia made a fuss of Bella, put a pasta dish in the microwave, and liberated a bottle of French Sauvignon Blanc from the fridge.

She paused a moment.

Sauvignon Blanc… a green-skinned grape variety from the Bordeaux region… from the French 'sauvage' or 'wild'.

"Well, we might not be in south-western France…"

It was a gorgeous evening – too nice to be inside – so

she poured a glass, went out onto the patio overlooking the silent vineyard, and lifted her glass to her nose.

Wet grass and passionfruit? Or maybe grapefruit?

She took a sip and left it on the tongue a moment.

Light bodied, good acidity, citrus, apple, and… gooseberry?

For some reason, the idea of visiting a French vineyard played out in her mind like an alluring travel film.

Come to Bordeaux! Enjoy the history, tradition, and stunning sunsets with local wine…

"What do you think, Bella? Bordeaux? Or how about Cote du Rhone or Burgundy? Or… Champagne?"

Bella was more interested in chewing a tennis ball.

Yes, the Champagne region, east of Paris. In relation to Kent, easier access than some of the farther-flung wine regions.

Would Gus like something like that?

No, he couldn't afford that kind of money.

Could she pay for him? She'd helped him pay for a few things lately, although she knew he wasn't comfortable with it.

Would she go with Gail then? It would be business-related, nothing more. She wouldn't simply be off having fun while Gus was working hard to keep his garage afloat.

And would she put Spencer off the idea of visiting her here in Maybrook? If indeed she should. After all, he was a fellow wine nut, nothing more.

17

An Informal Meeting

Just before lunchtime on Saturday, Olivia and Sue were strolling out of Colshot Lane bound for a bite to eat in the Royal Standard's beer garden.

"How's the volunteering going," Olivia asked. "The diary must be getting full."

Sue laughed. "Once you show a bit of willing, you get roped in more and more. Apparently, I'm already helping with hot food at the Christmas Bazaar."

"You love it though."

"I do – and it raises money for village causes."

Olivia approved. It was good for Sue to use retirement as a doorway into a new world.

"So, what's the latest with Luke?" Sue asked. "Any more changes of plan in the air?"

"He seems settled with Gus for now."

Olivia imagined a romantic Chinese takeaway with Gus… and with Luke sitting between them watching an arts documentary on TV.

"Sleeping on the sofa can't be much fun."

"Ah no, Gus has swapped. Luke has the Manager's Office."

"I see. Do you have any activities in mind? Things you could do with Gus and Luke?"

"Not really. I'm trying to think of something, but he's not going to say 'yay, an art exhibition'. I'm coming round to thinking it has to be the right thing at the right time with the right weather and all the stars lined up."

"What does Gus do with him?"

"Not much at the moment. He used to take him on adventures. Fishing, football…"

"That doesn't sound like Luke's thing at all."

"Gus came to realize that."

Gus greeted them with enthusiasm but was busy on a car and would work through lunch to make sure he got it back to a customer before the end of the day.

But that wasn't uppermost in Olivia's mind.

"Um… I've been thinking about visiting France. A vineyard, to be exact."

Gus seemed to be caught between nodding his approval and furrowing his brow.

Olivia continued, "It would probably be in August. A bit of business and pleasure. Fancy going with me?"

Gus shook his head.

"I can't commit to something like that, Liv. Sorry. Couldn't you go with one of your wine class friends?"

They left Gus to his work and continued to their lunch destination – with Olivia wondering if her relationship with Gus had reached its fullest extent. She lived at the vineyard, he lived above his garage. Was that it?

"Shame about France," said Sue. "I'd come myself, but I'm hardly a hard-core wine enthusiast."

"Sue – you're getting married. Maybe concentrate on a

honeymoon. Anyway, it's just an idea. Nothing concrete."

"Ken mentioned something about the parish council," said Sue. "Whether you might think about joining it."

"That's not going to happen."

Olivia was happy with her small band of friends. She had no appetite for engaging with an entire village.

"Cam thinks the council needs new blood."

"I'm sure they have someone in mind to co-opt."

"You could go up against their choice. You'd easily get ten people to support you."

"I don't know, Sue. I thought it might be a good idea to save the bridge, that's all."

"You're not serious then."

Olivia thought of Gus's commitment lecture to Luke.

"I did read up on it," she admitted. "One or two bits and pieces."

"What did you read? You'll need to be up to speed on what the parish council does. From what Cam tells me, they'll eat you alive if you're not."

"Sue, I'm not standing for election. However, from what I understand… ahem… their main business is making decisions and policy in the interest of the parish, which is enacted during meetings of the council."

"Hey, you swallowed the book."

"Yes, so, a parish council usually holds monthly meetings, although larger councils may have fortnightly meetings."

Sue laughed. And so did Olivia, before continuing.

"The council has a duty to provide the following facilities. Allotments."

She paused and Sue frowned.

"Yes, and…?"

"That's it. Allotment gardens for people to grow fresh produce. There's a duty to consider providing allotment gardens if demand is unsatisfied."

"I think you'll find they do a lot more than that."

"I think you'll find you're confusing duty with powers."

"Oh, very good, Olivia."

"They have the power to provide, maintain and manage many things, or they can contribute towards somebody else providing them. Shall I list them?"

"Go on."

"Okay, a community hall, outdoor recreational facilities, cemeteries and crematoria, litter bins, public seating areas, public toilets, a public clock, war memorials, parking facilities and, uh... the upkeep of the village green."

"We don't have a village green."

"Somebody should do something about that."

"Well, I'm impressed. That's quite a list. Mind you, it has to be said you're the most thorough person I know."

"I haven't finished."

"Oh."

"Parish councils have the right to be consulted by district and county councils on local planning applications, sewerage works, footpaths and rights of way."

"You certainly know your stuff."

"They can also use their powers to support arts and crafts, tourism, local voluntary organisations, public events, crime prevention..."

"Looking at your phone is cheating."

"...acquire or dispose of land, protection of unclassified highways and footpaths, and make byelaws in regard to pleasure grounds, cycle parks, and open spaces."

They paused outside the gate to the Royal Standard's beer garden.

"It would be great if you took up the challenge," said Sue.

Olivia was glad of her cousin's warmth and support. But

why would she? She wanted to save the bridge but joining the parish council seemed a step too far.

She pushed the gate open and headed for the side door into the pub.

At the bar, they were greeted by Annie, who looked as smart as ever in a thin lavender cardigan over a crimson blouse and with her hair freshly cut into a bob.

"Hello Annie," said Sue. "How was the break?"

"Lovely. Total relaxation by the sea. And the weather held up."

"Welcome back," said Olivia. "The Royal Standard's not the same without you."

Annie smiled and took their orders for sandwiches and a couple of shandies.

"So, what's new?" she asked.

"Olivia's thinking of joining the parish council," said Sue.

"Oh, that's—"

"Parish council?" Alan Curtis-Fisher's voice cut across from the other end of the bar. He was with Old Roper and two other men – and all clearly bought their unimaginative short sleeve shirts from the same store.

"I haven't actually decided," said Olivia.

"All are welcome to take an interest," said Curtis-Fisher in a 'don't bother' kind of way.

"We'll be outside," Olivia informed Annie.

She and Sue took their drinks into the beer garden and found a table.

"That's shaken them off," said Olivia.

"You spoke too soon," said Sue, indicating a pursuing group of four similarly attired, late middle-aged men.

Olivia said nothing but watched as they took an adjacent table.

"Do you know anything about parish councils?" said

Alan Curtis-Fisher, eyeing her.

"I know a little," said Olivia.

"Do you know how parish councils are funded?" asked Old Roper.

"Yes, by levying a precept, which comes from a portion of the district council tax paid by the residents of the parish. The thing is, I came here for lunch, not a pub quiz."

"Some of us dedicate ourselves to community life," said Alan Curtis-Fisher. "It's a full-time undertaking."

Olivia shrugged. "I'm only interested in finding a way to save the Hanway bridge. If you co-opted me, I'd focus solely on that."

"It's not a road safety issue," said Old Roper. "Whatever Steve Law says."

"It might be," Olivia insisted.

"Anyway, we already have one or two names seeking co-option. You'd be at the back of the line."

Sue bristled. "Olivia's not afraid of a by-election."

Olivia wondered – would she throw her hat into the ring? There were plenty of reasons not to. And when it came to the old stone bridge, was she even on the right side of the argument?

"What makes you think you could win an election?" said Old Roper with a hefty dose of disdain.

Olivia wasn't having that.

"What makes you think I can't?"

Alan Curtis-Fisher stood up, signalling that it was time for his troops to follow him back inside. As they did so, Annie came out with the sandwiches.

"I couldn't help overhearing that," she said as she placed the food before them.

"It's Olivia," said Sue. "She's an outsider causing trouble."

"It's the Hanway bridge," Olivia explained. "I don't

know if we can make it a road safety issue or not."

"So will you take them on?" asked Annie.

"Maybe."

While you're here though.

"Annie, could I ask you about someone from way back. Her name was Alice."

Olivia gave her what details she knew in the hope that Annie might be able to add something. But Annie looked uncomfortable.

"All I recall is that she was a lovely girl and yes, she was Gloria's relative. If you're saying she was a cousin's daughter, that sounds about right."

"I'm surprised she hasn't come up before," said Olivia. "We've had a few conversations about the past."

Annie thought for a moment before taking a seat alongside them.

"My sister…" she said, her voice lowered. "Years ago, her son, my nephew, was lost to us because of a stupid, meaningless nightclub fight in London. That kind of sadness is too painful. I run a pub. It's meant to be an escape for my customers, a bit of fun, a good laugh. A juicy bit of gossip, yes – but lingering on young lives and tragedy, no, never."

Annie stood up.

"I'm sorry," said Olivia.

Annie leaned in close.

"You know about Raymond – who helped Gloria at the vineyard?"

"Yes, the French guy," said Olivia. "He died before we came to Kent. They were friends."

Extremely good friends…

"Well, he knew Alice better than anyone. If you want to know more, you could try his brother-in-law."

18

The School Run

Monday began with a text. Gus had a migraine and so couldn't take Luke to school. It was something that came on rarely and would be gone in a day, but Olivia agreed it made driving unwise. So, at eight a.m., under a fabulous summer sky, she was outside Whitman Farm waiting for a precocious teen to arrive.

Assuming he did arrive.

No, he would be there soon. But what if turned up late? She didn't fancy trying to make up the time by speeding through the countryside.

She was pondering a call to Gus when the boy in question appeared at the top of the lane. He must have caught sight of her because he stopped and waited.

"Oh, sorry, your lordship," Olivia muttered.

She was soon in the car and pulling up to let him in. Over the weekend, she'd googled for things to do with an awkward, unhelpful, ungrateful teen. Well, just 'things to do' but, usefully, Canterbury was host to a modern art exhibition. They could go together and bond. Okay, semi-bond. Or quarter-bond.

"Any news on your bridge?" he asked as he settled in beside her.

"Are you sure you won't join me in trying to do something?"

"Too much work and other stuff. There's a society at school where we support environmental causes. I run it."

"Really?"

"Yes."

"So… school."

"We can go the other way if you like. It's only twenty minutes to the coast."

"And what would we do at the coast?"

"Swim to France?"

Olivia began to type the school's name into the sat-nav.

"No need," said Luke. "I'll show you the way."

"It has live traffic updates. Just in case."

"Are you aware that trust issues can poison a relationship?"

What relationship?

She turned left onto the main road.

"The coast's the other way," Luke pointed out.

"I'm not having an argument with my sat-nav."

She switched the radio on and selected something loud and modern. Twenty minutes of teen anthems wouldn't be intolerable. She even nodded her head to the beat. She would invite him to go to the art exhibition once they were almost at school. This would work out just fine.

"How can you listen to that?" Luke complained.

"Be my guest."

He selected a classical music station playing Mozart.

"You really didn't have to drive me," he insisted. "I could have walked."

"Walk? You wouldn't get there till lunchtime."

"I am a grain in a breeze, wafted high over countless miles. I am blown beyond these lands, beyond these rocky isles."

"Don't tell me… Sylvia Plath?"

"No, it's one of mine."

"You write poetry?"

"No, I did not run naked through the village, officer."

"Pardon?"

"Sorry, I thought I heard an accusation."

"No… sorry… I mean you obviously write poetry, which is great."

"My poetry's great?"

"I'm sure it is, but I meant it's great that you write it."

"My literature teacher says the same. Apparently, I'm tapping into my psyche to find ways of expressing myself. Emotional flowering."

"Yes, I can see that."

"A psychologist might say it's Freudian transference. Unrequited love thrust into a literary vehicle. You see I used the word thrust there? Freud would have jotted that down in his notebook."

Good grief…

"So, what subjects do you have today?"

"This and that. I'm thinking of doing those at university. Perhaps I'll get a doctorate in this and that. Or sinecure at Oxford. Professor of This and That."

Olivia sighed. She had only known him two weeks. It felt like two centuries.

"I'm thinking of standing for the parish council," she said – mainly as a preference to a period of silence or, worse, Luke talking rubbish. "I'm just trying to take it all in. I'm a bit lost, to be fair."

"Okay, so perhaps you should immerse yourself in the

milieu of it all?"

"I am. Did you know the 1894 Local Government Act created civil parish councils in England to have local oversight of civic duties in rural towns and villages?"

"You sound like you're giving a lecture."

"I practice in front of the mirror."

"Poor mirror."

"It helps me retain information."

"Nobody cares about that level of detail."

"I'd hate to have anyone accuse me of being an amateur."

"It's politics. Just tell them what they want to hear. You don't have to be passionate. Politicians generally fake it."

"Some of us hate to lie to people. That will be my strength."

"That will be your downfall."

"Yes, so… did you know that a minimum of three days' notice must be given for any meeting? The notice has to be placed in a 'noticeable place' in the parish, stating the time, date and venue."

"I've never noticed."

"Any item not mentioned on the agenda can only be debated if brought up by the public in attendance or via correspondence – but any resolution must be deferred to the next meeting."

"Your mirror gets all this? Maybe vineyards and politics don't mix. Your old job was probably a better match."

"The dark side of public relations?"

"Maybe I should get a job like that," Luke mused.

Olivia thought back to her final months at Prior Grove and to young Rob who sat in the opposite corner. He never wrote poetry – unless it was on the wall of the Gents' rest room.

"What kind of things did you get up to?" Luke asked.

"Oh, choosing which benefits to flag up. Maybe highlighting the points that benefitted our client. Maybe distracting people away from those that didn't."

"So, basically underhand stuff."

"The ends justify the means. That's what my boss used to say. It's a quote by Machiavelli."

"Pardon?"

"Haven't you read *The Prince*?"

"Yes, and he didn't say that. He said something like… give a prince credit for conquering, the means will always be considered honest."

"Moving on… I'm sure you'll end up working in a creative setting."

"Like a waiter in Hollywood?"

Olivia would have rolled her eyes but, with Gus's precious boy in the car, she chose to focus on the road. Of course, if they passed a lake, she would happily throw him in it.

But no… she wanted to help.

"While you're staying with Dad, I might volunteer to take you to school more often. Or pick you up. Also… there's a fantastic modern art exhibition on in Canterbury. I thought we might go together."

"You and Dad?"

"No, you and me."

Luke huffed. "I'm not really interested in somebody else's vision of what constitutes modern art."

"Right…" So much for art. She'd get him back to the bridge-saving idea. "Let's do something else together then."

"Do you know anyone in the creative industries?"

"Er… no, not as such. Look, why don't we both make an effort? I'll help with the school run; you help me save the bridge?"

He said nothing, but Olivia was determined.

"Luke?"

He stared out at the passing countryside.

"We could achieve something together," she added.

Luke's gaze remained fixed on the passing fields when he spoke.

"John Donne once said, 'No man is an island.' But, of course, many of us are."

"No problem," said Olivia. "We can fix that with a bridge."

19

Postcards, Letters, Photos

Olivia parked opposite a modest cottage in Ralston. In the road, a pigeon pecked at something someone had dropped. There was no High Street here; just some houses and a barn of sorts that had been converted into a farm shop and general store. Purple boot laces and all. There was no pub either, although there was one in the next village, which was a twenty-minute walk north. And no doubt thirty back. How long would it take to walk south to Maybrook? Forty minutes at a brisk pace? No wonder they never saw many Ralston folk.

She passed a cat sitting on a wall. The cat didn't move but tracked her progress, taking note.

"Hullo!" called John Bishop from his front doorstep. His late sister, Marje was married to Raymond Lafayette. Olivia had phoned in advance to explain that she lived at Whitman Farm and had become something of a student of its history.

A short while later, sitting with John in his warm, stuffy

lounge, mercifully refreshed by tea and chocolate chip cookies, she waited for him to finish his story about next door's cat, who she now knew better than John himself.

"Yes, so, Whitman Farm… the vineyard," she said in due course. "I know Raymond helped Gloria there for many years."

"Is it hot in here?" he asked.

Olivia could feel her blouse sticking to her back.

"A little, but…"

"I'll open a window."

She waited while he opened a window two inches. It did little but stir the warm air and dislodge the dust.

"So, Raymond?" Olivia prompted. "At Whitman Farm?"

"Did you know him?"

"No… but my partner, Gus Brody, used to look after his Renault. Gus said Raymond came here as a boy during the War. He said he was a nice man."

"Yes, well, he loved that vineyard like it was his own. A home from home, if you like. Well, he was lonely. His wife, my sister, passed away a long time ago."

Olivia sensed the loneliness in John too.

"Was he great friends with Gloria?" she asked after a pause.

"I believe so, yes, although he never went into much detail. From what I know, they shared two great passions. Wine and music."

"Music?"

"Yes, they were both musical. I think Gloria played the clarinet."

Olivia was a little surprised, but then chastised herself. Why shouldn't Gloria be musical? It was just that she'd never got that impression.

"Raymond played the violin, of course," said John. "He

was well known for it."

"Lovely." *Like Gus...* "Yes, so... I'm focussing a little on the people who worked at Whitman Farm before and after it became a vineyard. Did you ever hear of a girl called Alice?"

John shrugged. "I never visited the place, not even once. I met Gloria at a few functions over the years, but I didn't know her as such. Raymond always spoke well of them all though."

"That's nice to hear."

"He did leave a box of bits. Letters and stuff."

"Did he?"

"I offered it to his son, but he wasn't interested. He lives in New York. He's a lawyer – although he mentioned retiring soon. He has two grown up children, a boy and a girl. I'm not sure what they do for a living. He came over for the funeral."

"Yes, um... so Raymond left a few bits?"

"You're welcome to take a look."

"Thank you, that's very kind."

John disappeared into a back room and took a few minutes to find what he was looking for. Olivia heard a cupboard open and close and something clatter to the floor.

"He we are," he puffed as he came back into the room.

Olivia thanked him and opened the box on her knees. Inside were postcards, letters, and photos.

One of the photos, a polaroid, grabbed her attention. It was a sunny, outdoor shot of four people with musical instruments. Gloria was playing a clarinet. And Alice, perhaps aged sixteen, was playing a flute. A man and a woman had violins. Or perhaps one was a viola. A classical version of Folkie-Karaoke?

Olivia held it up for John to see.

"Any idea who the man and woman on the right are?"

John squinted. "Is that the musicians photo?"

"Yes."

"Raymond's on the right."

"Great. So… that's Great Aunt Gloria on the left, then Alice who worked there. Any idea who the woman between Alice and Raymond is?"

"No, sorry."

"You wouldn't know who took the photo?"

"No… no idea."

"Would you mind if I took a copy of this?"

"You can keep it if you want. Once I'm gone, I don't suppose anyone will be interested."

"No, it's fine. I'll use this."

Olivia pointed her phone's camera at the photo and captured a copy. Perhaps Ken would cast some light on the matter.

Or perhaps not.

"Right, well, thanks," she said.

But John came over and pressed the polaroid into her hand.

"Please, keep it. Your link to Gloria is a lot stronger than mine to Raymond."

*

The cemetery grounds were impeccably maintained with beautiful lawns and mature trees. Beneath a clear blue sky, it was a picture of peaceful rest, with the only sounds those of birdsong.

For a moment, Olivia's thoughts were for all those she had lost. She didn't feel despondent though. Time had given her the strength to breathe in and breathe out as the emotions flowed through her.

Her phone pinged. The daily poem was available. It was something she'd signed up to for some unknown reason. Perhaps to keep in Luke's good books? Or was it to find inspiration? That part rang true as she'd selected 'Inspirational' as her preferred category.

> 'Great tasks are but seldom given out,
> Great deeds are but for the few,
> Yet the little acts, not talked about,
> May need a faith as true.'

Olivia concurred with Ella Hines Stratton. Save the world?

No.

Save the bridge then?

Maybe not even that.

Her little act?

Wasn't that the ongoing business of belonging to Whitman Farm? She wanted to bring the history of the place out of the shadows and into the light.

She re-checked the Find a Grave details. The lure was there, undeniably, but she felt self-conscious. Silly, even. This was too much, surely… and yet she wanted to have that contact. Even if it were just to say hello and farewell.

It didn't take long to find Alice's grave.

She hadn't been expecting to see fresh pink carnations resting against the modest headstone though.

According to the date of birth inscription, Alice's birthday was two days ago.

"Hello Alice," said Olivia. "Lovely flowers. I wonder who left them…"

20

If California Can Do It…

Olivia drove to the Hallam Hotel on Wednesday wondering how a Down-From-Londoner might get elected to a parish council – and indeed if she should even try.

Should it come to an election, running a campaign would be a challenge. Some dark arts, for sure – on both sides. Perhaps she'd go over the top with posters of a placard-waving hero – herself – between a bulldozer and the bridge. She could post one on the official notice board.

Then again, perhaps not.

A few minutes before the class started, and while Hannah dealt with a phone call, Olivia found herself in a discussion with Spencer, Gail, and Norman about the Level Three course that would start in October.

"I'm definitely in," said Spencer.

"Me too," said Norman.

"It's tempting," said Olivia.

It seemed too early to be discussing it seriously, but the

others were all upbeat about being part of the ongoing journey.

"In other news…" said Gail, teasingly, "I've arranged a house-sit through a friend of a friend. It's a small vineyard in Champagne and two can go."

"Wow," said Spencer.

"I'm free," said Norman.

But Gail was looking to Olivia.

"It's sounds lovely," was all Olivia could manage. It needed more thinking time than a quick chat before class.

"Couldn't we all go?" asked Norman.

"It has to be a maximum of two," said Gail. "They would hate to think it was being used as a party venue."

"I don't blame them," said Olivia.

"Did you know it's the most northerly wine region in France?" said Gail.

"I did," said Spencer.

"It's to the east of Paris," said Gail, her eyes on Olivia, "so it's quite easy to get to. Did you know it's divided into three areas?"

"Er… no."

"The Montagne de Reims, the Côte des Blancs, and Vallée de la Marne."

Olivia was puzzled. Why was Gail trying to impress her?

"You seem to be well on top of it, Gail."

"Thanks. It's all about vines and méthode Champenoise. That's how they make champagne. It's fermented twice in the bottle."

Olivia knew that but just nodded.

"You have blended wines that give you vintage champagnes," Gail continued.

"That's from the same harvest," said Norman.

"You also get non-vintage," said Gail, "which is a blend of wines from different years."

Again, Olivia nodded patiently. Hopefully, Hannah would start the class soon.

"Non-vintage dry is popular," said Spencer, directly to Gail. "Brut means dry and it's usually the classic Champagne blend of Chardonnay, Pinot Noir and Pinot Meunier."

Olivia glanced at the clock.

"Blanc de Noirs means white from black," said Gail, directly to Olivia. "That's pinot noir and pinot Meunier. It's usually fruitier and more full-bodied."

"And then you get Blanc de Blancs," said Spencer, directly to Gail, "which means white from white. It's light-skinned grapes, usually Chardonnay, and it gives you a light, dry Champagne."

"Is French always the best wine?" asked Norman.

Hannah came in at that moment.

"Funny you should say that, Norman," she said, raising her voice to bring in the rest of the class. "Regarding the reputation of French wine, is anyone familiar with the Judgment of Paris?"

"I thought that was Greek," said Spencer.

"Yes, but beyond the Greek mythological figure of Paris, there was a wine-tasting event in 1976 that changed the world of wine. Up until then, American wines were considered inferior – and I mean like a hotdog is inferior to a gourmet meal. Are you sure you haven't heard of it?"

"I'm just googling it now," said Norman.

Olivia was annoyed.

"I'm not googling it," she said with her focus fixed on Hannah. "What happened?"

"I've got it now," said Norman.

"Yes, what happened, *Hannah*," said Gail, pointedly.

"Okay, so French and American winemakers went head-to-head in a wine-tasting contest run by a British wine merchant called Steven Spurrier. He used the American bicentennial as an excuse to pit established, world-class French wines against the new kid on the block – wine coming out of California."

"Yes, 1976, it was," said Norman. "The American bicentennial."

"Um… so, wines were judged by a top-class panel, and everyone expected a French clean sweep."

"The constitution was signed in 1776," said Norman, by now to no one.

"First up, the white wines were judged in a blind tasting. California won three out of the four top places."

"Wow," said Gail.

Olivia thought the same.

"Everyone was shocked," said Hannah, "and Mr Spurrier developed a sudden panic that the Americans might also win the more prestigious red contest – which would be earth-shattering."

"The United States Declaration of Independence was originally known as the Unanimous Declaration of the thirteen United States of America. It was adopted by the Second Continental Congress meeting in Philadelphia, Pennsylvania, on July 4, 1776…"

"Thanks, Norman," said Hannah. "We have the utmost respect for Independence Day, but shall we stick to wine?"

"Did they win?" asked Gail.

"Right, so… aware of the ramifications, the judges were on guard against demoting the reputation of the French vineyards. However, it was a blind tasting and the wine they chose as the world's number one red was… drum roll… a Californian Cabernet."

"Wow," said Gail, again.

"It changed everything and opened the door to the New World."

"Amazing," said Olivia.

If California could take on French wine, then so could she. But that wasn't the thought uppermost in her mind as she smiled at Gail and pondered Champagne – the region, not the drink.

"Now," said Hannah, "Cabernet Sauvignon is our best known and most grown red wine grape. From France it has spread everywhere from North America to Australia and New Zealand. As for Cabernet Sauvignon itself – it came about thanks to a chance crossing of Cabernet Franc and Sauvignon Blanc in the 17th Century…"

*

After the class, Olivia and the others spilled out to the hotel lobby where conversations ran on amid the goodbyes. Olivia broke off promptly though and headed for her car.

Spencer was right beside her.

"I'm the Polo," she said.

"Then that's me next to you."

She wasn't good at identifying cars, but it looked like it might be a Toyota.

"Far to go?" she asked.

"In life or to get home?"

She smiled. "To get home."

"I recently moved to a place just outside Ashford, so it's not far. How about you?"

They had reached their cars and she didn't want to name Maybrook.

"Not far."

"I was based in Rochester for twenty years," he said. "Wonderful history there. I never settled down though. Never found The One."

"Oh."

"Is that an interest of yours?"

Finding the One?

"Er…"

"History's a big thing with me."

Ah.

"Yes, history is amazing."

Amazing? Grow up.

"Did you notice Rochester accidentally lose its city status?"

Olivia had no idea what he was talking about, but she quite liked the way he said it.

"No, I can't say I did."

"Eight centuries. Count them… and in all that time Rochester was Kent's second cathedral city."

Olivia knew that Canterbury was Kent's only city, and that the title came with the cathedral.

"What happened?" she asked, keen to get away, and yet happy to linger a moment longer.

"In 1998, a bunch of… let's call them local busybodies… decided to change the way the area's councils were set up. They merged the entire district into the Medway Unitary Authority. As part of it, Rochester became the only British city ever to lose its status."

"That's a bit unfortunate," said Olivia.

"I sometimes wonder if we'd be better off letting children make our local authority decisions. At least it would be fun."

"I'm sure they didn't mean to lose a city."

"You're too generous. It was four years before they even noticed they'd lost it. They've been appealing to the Government ever since to let the Medway Unitary Authority become a city instead. So far, no luck – which is good, because they don't deserve any."

It made Olivia think. If all those high-ranking officials

and representatives could lose a city…

Why assume Maybrook Parish Council knows what it's doing?

"Well, I'll be off then," said Spencer. "Unless…?"

But Olivia was already in her car and waving him goodbye.

21

Viv & Liv

Olivia pulled up outside Viv's place on a warm, sunny Thursday afternoon. It was a large old house with white rendered walls and black window frames that most likely dated back more than a century.

She thought back to that first time they met at Ramsey's winery and how it had seemed a fun idea to have a Viv and Liv episode. A flash of doubt raced through her mind, but she dismissed it. She was *not* too self-conscious to act silly in a video. And she didn't care who saw it.

She got out of the car and grabbed her straw hat off the passenger seat.

"Hellooooo!"

Viv was already at the front door, dressed in a rainbow poncho and waving a multi-bangled hand.

Once they had hugged, Olivia entered a world of Bohemian décor and fittings.

"I just had a text from my daughter, Ellie," said Viv. "She'll be here soon. She's a sixth former and they get home study time."

"Oh great."

"Tea? Coffee?"

"Tea would be lovely, thanks."

She stood in the hallway while Viv went into the kitchen.

"Do you take sugar?"

"No, just milk, thanks."

A photo of a happy border collie with a tennis ball in its jaws stared back at her from the wall. There were words below.

'Darling Rosie, you ran for miles along the shore at Folkestone, and for miles along the peak of the Downs overlooking so much of Kent. And when you slept, tired and satisfied, you continued to run (your active face and twitching legs told us your dreams, my girl). There's a tennis ball, torn and shredded. It still bounces well and it's still yours even though you've been gone for half my life. It will remain here always, just like my memories of you.'

Viv reappeared and directed her to a rear patio bursting with potted flowering plants before disappearing back inside.

'Won't be a mo with the tea," she said before disappearing back inside.

Olivia admired the vista – the orchard, the vineyard, the fields beyond… and nearby, a bee at work.

A teenage girl came out to join her.

"You come to do a video?" she asked flatly.

Olivia found her attitude quite surly, even for a teenager.

"Yes, we discussed it a while back… and here I am."

"Nobody watches them."

"I'm sure it's a couple of hundred."

"You can't get the advertisers interested with a couple

of hundred. If you have millions of followers, you can earn big bucks."

Olivia liked her less and less but tried not to show it.

"That's easier said than done," she said with a smile.

"I wanna be an influencer in beauty products."

"Is that where the followers are?"

The girl laughed. "Well, they're not watching daft old women doing songs and poems, are they."

The girl went back inside, passing Viv, who was returning with a smile and two mugs of tea.

"Here we are…"

Olivia accepted a mug and thanked her.

"Your daughter seems quite forthright."

"That's not my daughter. That's Sadie. I'm a foster carer."

"Oh."

Olivia began to wonder when she'd developed this gift for snap judgements and wrong conclusions.

"Troubled times for her," said Viv. "Obviously, I can't say much – confidentially and all that. She's been here a few weeks and we've managed to settle things down a bit, so all's as well as can be."

"I see…"

"My daughter should be home soon."

"So, you're a foster-carer… I suppose we don't really know much about each other outside of vines."

"No – you go first."

"Oh, right."

Olivia gave a speedy history of her time in London, her time with her ex, her chance to take on Great Aunt Gloria's vineyard alongside Sue and Milo, and her current situation with Gus.

Viv smiled. "My potted history is being a single mum who ended up living at her uncle's place and turned two acres of his orchard into a vineyard."

"And foster-caring."

"And that, yes."

Their conversation was interrupted by the arrival of Ellie, who was brief but courteous with a hello and a wave before attempting to disappear again.

"Not so fast," said Viv. "This is Liv…"

"You're not forming a double act, are you?"

"For one video only – yes," said Viv. "At least, for now."

"Do you like your mum's videos?" Olivia asked.

"No comment."

"Oh."

"Let's just say I get plenty of feedback at school."

Olivia could imagine it.

"So, let's do the video," said Viv. "I was thinking of a little song and dance."

Olivia suddenly felt too self-conscious for singing and dancing. Perhaps once Ellie had departed…

"Ellie will be chief camera operator and director as usual."

Ellie frowned. "I'm meant to be reading about Neville Chamberlain's policy of appeasement." She turned to Olivia. "Be warned. Mum doesn't care that hundreds of kids at school will have a good laugh."

"Take no notice," said Viv. "You have to be a mother to understand she doesn't mean a word of it."

That stung Olivia.

"Um, actually…"

She grasped for the right words.

"You'll do the video…?" said Viv, looking a little crestfallen.

"No, sorry. I'm…"

"Oh, are you sure?"

"Yes, um…"

Olivia made her excuses and left.

22

Lightweight

Coming back along Potter's Lane after a walk to the bridge with Bella, Olivia was enjoying the early evening sunshine.

"I reckon we've earned a cool drink when we get home," she said. "I think one of us should have Sauvignon Blanc. What do you think?"

Bella nudged Olivia's hand.

"Hey, it's me who decides when the treats are handed out."

Bella licked her lips.

Olivia gave her a treat.

She still felt bad about Viv. Shouldn't she be proud of her friend's efforts? Wasn't embarrassment the preserve of the teenager? How could she guide Luke when her concerns about looking a right twit had derailed a potentially important friendship?

Was she a lightweight?

Her phone pinged. It was a text from Katy.

The parish council was planning to co-opt Jason

Brunton, the fifty-something son of octogenarian Colin, who created the vacancy when he stood down due to declining health.

Despite Jason's credentials and backing, Olivia felt the pressure to oppose him. It didn't help that she could picture him as a Roman gladiator, like Russell Crowe in that movie. She could hear his mighty roar. 'Stand aside! I am Son of Colin!'

Maybe she'd need a persona to counter him. Olivia Holmes in a bikini made of vine leaves. 'I am Wine Woman. Why don't you fizz off!'

No, there didn't need to be any hostility. And he'd probably forgotten it was her dog who stole his bacon baguette that time.

As she and Bandit Dog made their way home to the sound of birdsong, she thought about a possible election. And a possible trip to France. And she wondered, as an outsider in Maybrook, which one she should be focusing on.

At the end of Potter's Lane, Ken and Beano were coming along. They said their hellos, but she didn't suppose he'd want to talk about cemetery flowers. She knew he'd feel that Gloria and Alice were best left alone.

There was something though.

"I've got an old photo, Ken." She showed him the musical group snap on her phone, carefully avoiding pointing at Gloria or Alice. "Do you know who this woman might be?"

He peered, perhaps too casually.

"Not sure."

"It might be someone local."

"Well… it might be Judy Shore."

"Oh… you're right." Olivia knew her from the greengrocers.

"Good."

"I don't suppose you know who might have taken the photo?"

"I don't," he said, sounding pretty fed up with her questioning. "I try to keep out of other people's business."

Ouch.

It didn't take much guesswork to know she was well on the way to spoiling an important friendship.

"Sorry, Ken."

Ken seemed to reflect on it for a moment. Olivia remained silent.

"Gloria's cousin…" he said heavily. He took another moment. "She used to encourage Alice to come over and earn a bit of pocket money, so that explains that. And they all had an interest in music, which explains the instruments. All I can add is… may they rest in peace."

"Yes, absolutely," said Olivia, backing off.

"So… still thinking of standing for the parish council?" he asked.

"Possibly."

"I've heard the district council closed the bridge to cyclists and pedestrians because the cracks might be worse than previously thought. So, no chance of a preservation order."

"So that's it?"

"I expect so – but I know you. If you think something's important, you won't give up."

*

Just before five, Olivia hesitated outside Shore's the greengrocers, where the year before, Judy Shore told her about the Whitman family's connection to Maybrook dating back four centuries.

I can't do this…

But Judy appeared at the window and waved.

Olivia took a fortifying breath and entered.

A few minutes later, sitting in the back room, sipping hot tea, she explained her interest in Alice as part of Whitman Farm's story and showed her the musicians' photo.

"I remember it well. It was informal but we met for practice and played at a few fetes – that kind of thing. It didn't last."

"Cam told me Alice was Gloria's relative – possibly a cousin's daughter."

"Yes, I think you're right. I didn't know her all that well. I think Ken's the best person to ask. I'm sure he went to the funeral."

Olivia wasn't surprised – the inevitability of Ken knowing plenty hardly needed a fanfare.

"As I said, I'm looking into Whitman Farm's story. To be honest though, it's hard to know where the farm's history starts and people's privacy ends. I went to the cemetery. There were flowers for Alice's birthday. I don't know if I should ask if anyone knows who left them."

"It sounds like a private matter to me."

"I agree… so you don't think it might have been Ken?"

"You'd have to ask him."

"I can't. He thinks I'm poking my nose into other people's business."

"Yes, well…"

"Sorry, you're right."

"It's okay, but I really don't know much. I heard Gloria's cousin had a difficult pregnancy – high blood pressure, so she was bedbound. Gloria stayed with her, which worked out because Gloria was having a difficult time with Charlie."

"Do you remember who took the photo?"

"Alice's boyfriend, I expect. I don't remember his name. First love, I think. I don't think it lasted."

Olivia wondered about the boyfriend – but only for a moment. This wasn't about tracking down every person who had ever known Alice Osborne. It was about possibly reclaiming her as part of the Whitman Farm family. But if that meant upsetting Ken, then maybe she'd taken it as far as she could.

She thanked Judy and left for home wondering if Alice was Gloria's daughter. She knew Ken and Gloria had a fling in the early 60s. He once told her it was when Gloria and Charlie bought Whitman Farm from Gloria's family. Ken helped them move in, except Charlie was busy elsewhere. Ken insisted it wasn't anything like loose morals – just long-held, long denied love.

Olivia often wondered why he shared things with her that he never breathed to anyone else. Everything was telling her this was about Ken and Gloria, but it was none of her business. And it wasn't right to put two and two together and make five at Gloria's expense.

A short while later, on the patio at Whitman Farm, she studied the polaroid photo once more.

And something clicked.

The rear edifice of the house, to the right of the kitchen, by the corner where she, Sue and Milo first emerged from the weeds down the side path to set eyes on the vineyard. It was a fond and vivid memory. But…

She held the photo up at arm's length.

Between the kitchen window and the corner.

The musicians.

Right there…

Her face broke into a smile that was both pleased and a little sad. More than four decades ago, they stood there enjoying the sunshine on a summer's day. A perfect moment, captured in time.

She wondered what melody might have filled the air… and if she could ask Ken if Alice was Gloria's daughter? Or his daughter? Or the cousin's daughter? Or would she simply put the photo in Gloria's box of things and bid Alice farewell?

23

Buddy, Can You Spare a Day… or Two?

Weatherwise, late June was disappointing, with rain and wind coming in off the Atlantic, but things changed during the first week of July with raging heat wafting up from Africa. That was now subsiding, and Kent was returning to the more tolerable norms of an English summer.

It was a Saturday morning and Olivia was dog-walking with a slight hangover – courtesy of a lengthy Friday visit from Gail. There had been lots of talk about France, lots of giggles while practising essential French phrases, and lots of French wine consumed in the name of research.

Bella, meanwhile, was on the way to becoming a dog transformed – so long as the praise kept coming, including stops at Ken's for extra praise.

From the old bridge, Olivia could see Alan Curtis-Fisher with the surveyor at Forest Edge. Parish council business, no doubt. She decided against intervening.

Instead, she and Bella walked along the bank for a couple of hundred yards downstream before coming back.

Passing Cam's place on the way home, she glanced over to make sure no post was sticking out of the letterbox. He and Sue were away in Brighton for a long weekend and wouldn't be back until Monday afternoon. Milo had texted his shock and outrage that two old timers should be up to that kind of thing. He added that he was jealous.

Back at home, Olivia set Bella up with water and some crunchy dog snacks.

"You have my permission to take a nap… oh, you mean that was your plan anyway?"

She ruffled Bella's neck and kissed the top of her head. "See you soon."

Reaching the main road, she squinted against the sun to Gus's garage a little way up on the other side of the road. She could make out Luke… and a woman. He was wiping her car windscreen.

For Olivia, the relationship with Luke had drifted into a 'treading water' situation – a degree of effort but no visible movement in any direction. He was still living with Gus and going to school, but she only saw him for brief periods.

Arriving at the forecourt, it occurred to her that Luke was flirting. But that couldn't be right. The woman had to be at least thirty.

Gus emerged from the garage with some paperwork. He smiled but remained focused on his customer who, it transpired, was thanking him for a successful M.O.T. on her four-year-old Renault.

She gave Luke a couple of coins before driving away.

"Me and Luke are having dinner at Beth's," said Gus.

This got an eye-roll from Luke, but Olivia was happy that his aunt was still in the picture. Maybe he'd stay with her for a few days. Or a week, even.

Gus went back inside, leaving Luke and Olivia facing each other like two gunfighters beneath a hot sun.

"I hear your bridge doesn't have long," he said. "Goodbye and ka-boom."

"It'll be knocked down not blown up."

"Pity – it could've gone viral with an explosion."

"So… Aunt Beth's tonight."

"Yawn."

"It's important."

"To Dad, yes."

Olivia was annoyed.

"Your dad only wants the best for you."

"Oh right."

"He's your father, Luke."

"Isn't that a line from Star Wars?"

"I can still hear you," said Gus from inside.

"We need to get you sorted."

"We?"

"Your aunt, your dad… you need to get everything sorted so that you're free to focus on school and the things you love doing. Piano, art, literature…"

We won't mention arguing and being awkward.

"I have disappointing news," said Luke. "I'm not doing great at them."

"You do interesting things. Do them to the best of your ability."

"And that'll keep me interesting?"

"I wish I'd worked hard at the things I enjoyed."

"You didn't?"

"No."

"So, you're not interesting?"

Bloody cheek.

"Look, if I do a final bit of campaigning to save the

bridge, would you help? I think it's a good idea to raise awareness."

"I'm busy."

"I know, but…"

A car pulled up a few feet away and the window wound down to reveal Alan Curtis-Fisher.

"Is it right you still plan to block us co-opting Colin's son?"

She'd made it known she hadn't ruled anything out.

"Let's wait and see."

"Jason gives us continuity. He's lived in the village most of his life."

"That's not the point. My family was here four hundred years ago."

"Yes, but your branch left."

Olivia was trying to work out an answer, but the window hummed shut and Alan Curtis-Fisher drove off.

She turned to Luke.

"Are you sure you can't spare some time? I just want to knock on a few doors. My experience is that it helps to look like I have a team behind me."

"You plus me doesn't equal a team."

"You're forgetting Sue – but our combined age is over a hundred. We need you."

"To bring the average age down?"

"To help us when I make the point about the bridge affecting the future of our young people. You could look close to tears."

"I've got some reading to catch up on. Sorry."

"I just need a couple of days of your time."

"Days?"

"Hours then."

"I've got a lot on."

"Luke, you're bright and… actually, you're super bright

and yet you seem to carry the weight of the world on your shoulders."

"You're confusing me with Atlas. Did you know he turned to stone when he looked at the Gorgon? A rock actually. No, a mountain, now I think of it."

Gus came out of the garage.

"Time out, people. How about some coffee?"

Olivia considered it but she needed a proper break.

"Sorry, I need a few things from the High Street. Have a good time at Beth's."

As she headed off, a car came alongside, following her slowly.

A kerb-crawler?

The window wound down to reveal Alan Curtis-Fisher once more.

"How about we clear the air?"

Olivia wasn't sure what he meant, but he continued.

"There's a little thing on later at the Old Hall pub. It's just a few friends talking about village matters on an informal basis. If you're serious, be there at seven. Who knows – you might change a few minds?"

Olivia nodded. At last, sanity ruled.

24

Alan's Casual Country Folk

Olivia was getting ready to go out. It would be a long, warm July evening, so she opted for a glittery blouse and comfortable jeans. A quick touch of make-up and she was ready for a burger and a beer with the best of them.

"Sorry to ruin your Saturday night, Bella, but this might be a good opportunity to get things going in the right direction."

Bella was sprawled across the hall floor.

"A spot of grown-up chat, a touch of ironing things out, a dash of acceptance…"

With her bag over her shoulder, she left the house and strolled up Colshot Lane. Although it was almost seven o'clock, it felt like late afternoon.

Reaching the main road, a noisy old car leaving the village roared by heading north. She walked on, passing Gus's garage on the other side. The main light in the lounge was on – Gus's security system – although it wouldn't be much of a deterrent until after dark. She silently wished him and Luke a good evening at Beth's. Hopefully, things would be a lot clearer in the morning.

At the Old Hall pub, she pushed the door open and entered. They were all there, at the bar, including Alan Curtis-Fisher, who gave her a hearty smile.

"You came – excellent. Come and join us."

She did so.

"You said it was informal," she said.

"The discussions – they are informal. Absolutely."

"The dress code isn't," said Old Roper, seemingly fresh from his annual bath.

"You know Jason," said Alan. He ushered Jason, Son of Colin to stand beside her – him, like the rest of the men, in a dinner suit with frilly shirt and bowtie.

"Here," said Old Roper, handing her a bottle of cider.

A flash. And another.

Photos… of casual Olivia with a bottle of cider standing alongside smart Colin and his small, classy sherry.

Great…

"Let's talk," said Alan.

"Why are you all dressed up?" she asked, putting the cider down.

"It's a small, yearly thing we do. We meet here to sink a few quick ones, then we walk a few yards to the Old Hall for dinner with the ladies. They're over there now, no doubt knocking back the Prosecco."

"How are you settling into the village?" Jason, Son of Colin asked.

This wasn't a drink; it was a trap. She needed a way to fight back.

"Very well, thanks," she said. "I haven't noticed you at any parish council meetings…?"

"You've lost me, Octavia."

Just then, Katy Law came in, looking great in a sleek

black evening gown. She was with a man in full dinner attire.

Olivia headed straight for her.

"Lovely to see you, Katy."

"Hello, Olivia. Meet my husband, David."

They swapped hellos but Olivia was keen to latch on to the only other female present.

"Can I get you guys a drink?" she offered.

"I'm just passing through," said Katy. "There's a thing going on in the hall…"

Olivia waited for her to say a brief hello to a few of her fellow council members. Then she followed Katy out through the back door.

"Sorry about that, Olivia. Joining the ladies is a bit old-fashioned, obviously… why are you here?"

"Alan Curtis-Fisher ambushed me."

"Ah… well, there is some news. The district council's discussing the bridge this week. I'm not expecting much though."

"Right. Oh well…"

"Are you going back in with them?"

"Probably not."

"There's one person it might be worth singling out. Robin Welland. He has connections to the district council. On the downside, he's Kent's most boring man – which is strange, because he's a historian and wears red glasses. They're always interesting on TV."

"Be honest – is this hopeless?"

Katy shrugged. "Probably. Unless there's a strong argument at the local level."

"So, be nice to Alan?"

"Yes. Good luck."

Olivia watched Katy disappear into the Old Hall and wondered – why care about any of this? She then took stock of a pertinent fact – in 1604, her ancestors, Josiah and Jeremiah Whitman contributed to the hall's construction.

That's why, pea-brain.

She turned to the pub of the same name.

Inside, she spotted Robin Welland talking with a fellow suit-wearer.

No point beating about the bush.

"They changed the law in '74," Robin explained to his colleague.

"Sounds like the start of a Bob Dylan song," said Olivia, picking up her cider and joining them without an invite. "They changed the law in '74… the right to brew hooch was no more."

She took a swig from the bottle.

Robin Welland didn't look impressed.

"The new law in 1974 meant that a parish council could pass a resolution to declare its area a town."

"Yes, I know. I can't see Maybrook being a town though."

"Why not?" said Robin's colleague.

"Well… it's a lovely village, obviously."

"It's a growing village," said Robin.

"If we become a town, we could have a mayor," said his friend.

"Yes, why not," said Olivia. "Shall we draw straws?"

Robin bristled. "The council chairperson would automatically become mayor."

"You want to be careful," said the friend in a serious tone. "Some parishes become cities."

"I hardly think Maybrook is about to rival London," said Olivia.

"The parish would require an Anglican cathedral to become a city," said Robin. "Like Chichester and Ely…

and indeed Salisbury if I'm not mistaken."

"On another historical point," said Olivia, "my family were here four hundred years ago. Not in this pub, obviously, although… well, two of them have their names on the plaque, so they might have come in for a pint… assuming there was a pub here at that time… was there?"

"Er…" Robin looked to his friend for help but having enjoyed enough history, he'd slipped away.

He turned back to Olivia.

"Yes, so… my specialism is Roman Britain. I've written a book about Canterbury."

"Yes, but pubs in Maybrook…?"

"I believe the Royal Standard was the first – an inn with stables, ideally situated for those passing through. It's not my area of expertise though."

"What's your opinion on the Hanway bridge?"

"It's a modest example of that kind of bridge. It was built in the 19th Century."

"1867."

"There, you know more than I do."

"So, what's your opinion on trying to save it."

"If we're to have direct vehicular access from Forest Edge, and indeed from Ralston, we need a new bridge."

"You know people at the district council. If you were to support the campaign to save it…"

"There's really no reason to. Sometimes, things simply outlast their use. The really interesting Kentish history is Roman. Julius Caesar named the county as Cantium, and the local people as the Cantiaci. We were ruled from Durovernum Cantiacorum – modern day Canterbury. When I say 'we', I mean the people of Kent."

Olivia smiled and noted how Spencer at wine class made history sound interesting, whereas Robin made her brain cells shrivel.

While he had more to say about the Cantiaci, Olivia was drawn to Alan Curtis-Fisher guffawing like a donkey at something or other.

She turned back to Robin.

"I don't suppose history reveals any illegal goings-on with the Curtis-Fisher family?"

"Alan is a pillar of the community and a very good friend of mine."

"Talking about me?" said Alan Curtis-Fisher, moving in on their conversation so that he stood alongside Robin to face the newcomer, two against one.

"Do you know Alan?" Robin asked.

"A little."

Then Old Roper joined them to make it three against one.

"We don't want a fight," said Alan Curtis-Fisher. "I'm sure we can find a way to help you see our very reasonable point of view."

"I'm just trying to find a way to save the bridge. It looks like I may have come to the wrong place."

"Maybrook?" said Alan Curtis-Fisher. "Not at all. We welcome all new arrivals."

"I'd better be going." She handed Old Roper her half-finished bottle of cider. "Thanks for the drink."

*

Olivia was home early and enjoying Bella's welcome – it ranked as a 'you've been away a whole year!'

"Guess what, Bella… Julius Caesar had a holiday home in Colshot Lane. Who'd have thought?"

She freed one of two emergency frozen pizzas she kept in case Luke ever showed up. While waiting for the oven to do its work, she wandered into the lounge – where

Gloria's box of stuff caught her eye.

A moment later, she was sifting absently through the contents. She then placed Steve's box file alongside it on the coffee table. She had the photo of Alice as a musical teenager, and the newspaper photo. Pieces of a puzzle of a life.

Later, after she'd eaten and watched some TV, she took Bella for a walk. They stopped at Ken's to say hello and check on him. Bella insisted.

At the stone bridge, in the last light of the day, Olivia watched Vineyard Viv's latest video – a poem about summer. The final lines were:

'My love of summers and my summers of love,
The green below, the blue above,
Those long hot days were my best friend,
Young forever, no thought of an end.'

Olivia smiled and wondered – did Alice have a love of summers and summers of love? She hoped so.

Her phone pinged.

It was a text from Gus.

'Luke staying with Beth tonight. She'll drop him back to me after Sunday lunch. I'll be home 10 p.m. Hint, hint xx'

Olivia smiled. Aunt Beth and her man had enjoyed plenty of hint, hint time recently. That said, Olivia's day felt too finished. Besides, they would have six weeks together during the school holidays, when Luke would be hundreds of miles away in Scotland.

She texted back.

'Sorry, a bit tired xx'

She thought for a moment. This probably wasn't the best way for a relationship to thrive.

She texted again.

'I'll pop over tomorrow morning at ten for coffee. Hint, hint xx'

Gus texted straight back: 'xxxxxxx'

She chuckled and spent a moment imagining it.

25

Olivia's Taxi Service

Olivia was parked opposite the school on Monday afternoon, waiting to collect Luke. She was five minutes early and the street was quiet. Chopin on Classic FM was playing softly at low volume.

She reflected on Sunday with Gus. A lovely day. Relaxing. No disturbances. In fact, Gus had made it her day, preparing lunch and playing her African Queen DVD. He got every detail right. Later, when she was back at home, preparing for bed, he texted her: 'I'm sure things will work out. Your patience means a lot. Love Gus xx'

Activity across the road brought her back to the present. The first students were emerging through the school gates. She looked for Luke, but he wasn't among them.

He'd stayed with Beth overnight and had gone directly to school from there. According to Gus, Beth was looking to make a change in her own life. She was thinking of moving to be with her man who was based in Royal

Tunbridge Wells – a forty-five-minute drive from Beth's current abode. Luke wasn't keen on switching to a school in Royal Tunbridge Wells, where he'd be 'stuck' if he didn't like it. It seemed like further dinners and discussions would be needed to sort it out.

She looked to the school gates again.

There was still no sign of him.

With just two weeks before schools broke up for summer, she was determined they should have one final go with the bridge campaign. With hordes of children coming through the school gates, she felt like leaping out of the car and yelling, "Who's with me?" So far it was Sue and Katy; both of them possessing a superpower – the ability to lift their butt off the sofa and fight for a better outcome. But what better outcome?

According to Katy, a cracked bridge could mean the council weren't insured should there be an incident. That's why they had closed it to everyone. Olivia thought a full structural survey would be the right way forward but, apparently, there was no money for a survey on a structure that was due for demolition.

Olivia looked for Luke again. There was still no sign of him, although… wasn't that boy one of the few she'd seen talk to him?

She wound down the window and called out.

"Hello!"

He looked over, not quite understanding.

"I'm waiting for Luke Collingwood."

"Oh."

"He's not staying behind or anything?"

"I don't think so."

"I know he runs the environmental group."

"Huh?"

"You're not a member?"

The boy came over with a confused look on his face.

"You're not a member?" Olivia repeated. "Of Luke's environmental group?"

"Sorry, I'm not sure what you mean," he said before hurrying away, no doubt in line with the school's policy on weirdoes in cars.

For Olivia though, it more or less confirmed that Luke wasn't quite the eco-warrior he'd suggested.

A moment later, he crossed the road and got in alongside her.

"Luke, I was just speaking with a friend of yours. Are you sure you run an environmental group? He didn't seem to think so."

"And good afternoon to you too, Olivia. It's lovely to see you."

"Why do you make stuff up?"

"Why do you say things to those who'll spread it around the school and make my life even less pleasant?"

Olivia considered it.

"You're right. Sorry. School is an unforgiving place. I should know that."

She put the car in gear and pulled away, hoping the situation would naturally sort itself out without too much pain. But then she spotted the boy a little way down the street.

Slowing alongside, she wound down the window and yelled, "Luke's co-leading a campaign to save an old bridge in Maybrook. We couldn't do it without him."

The boy looked no less puzzled by this than their earlier encounter. Luke meanwhile was incandescent as they drove away.

"Why can't you just…"

"Provide a taxi service?"

"Yes, and on that score, why don't we cancel it. This

isn't working for me."

"Your dad can't drop you and pick you up every day. And he can't afford an actual taxi either. You'll just have to put up with me."

"Brilliant."

Olivia took a breath. This couldn't go on.

"Luke, I'm doing my best to help, so stop being a jerk."

"That's not a word I'd associate with you?"

"Trust me, I was tempted by a different one. Anyway, two more weeks and you'll be off to Scotland."

And I'll be with your dad.

"Yes, well, on that matter, I've decided to stay with Dad for the summer holidays."

"What?"

"It's quite straightforward."

"What happened to Scotland?"

"As far as I know, it's still there."

"Luke!"

"A change of plan, that's all. Scotland's out, Dad's in."

Olivia felt a pang of guilt. Ever since losing Jamie, she had cherished the idea of having a child. And yet here was a 'child' hovering on the edge of her life and he was a right pain in the backside.

26

T-Shirt Guy vs Spartacus

Olivia was in her bedroom, getting ready to go out.

"I used to be the woman who sat in the corner," she told Bella. "My desk was by the fire exit. No, I know that doesn't seem right, but that's how it was. No, I know you can't flippin' believe it, but I used to hope things might work out… that maybe some power might see to it…"

She smiled – some power *had* seen to it. Whitman Farm had fired up her passion for life. But once fired up, was passion lifelong? Or was it a fire that required feeding over and over?

"Have I let things slip?" she asked her dog.

She wondered – had she been throwing the odd twig on the fire rather than a series of logs?

"I spent years waiting for life to happen, Bella. Not anymore."

She dug something particular out of the wardrobe. A Prior Grove work outfit.

"Yes, the professional look."

Once she was dressed, she went downstairs. In the lounge, Gloria stared at her from her frame.

Olivia returned her gaze.

"I'm standing for the parish council, Gloria. Don't laugh, this is total commitment. Yes, I know I've only been here eighteen months. And yes, I know it's an all-new total commitment."

She stuffed her laptop into a shoulder bag and set off.

Five minutes later, she arrived at Gus's to find him sweeping up prior to locking up for the day.

"You look smart," he said.

"Thanks. Shall I make some tea?"

"Look, um… there's another option come up. Actually, it's been there all along. It's not one I like or want, but… a mate of mine has a garage in Maidstone. He needs a mechanic."

"I see."

"I could sell this place and work for him. I'd rent a place near Luke's school."

Olivia wasn't at all happy.

"It makes sense, I suppose. To live near the school."

"I wouldn't get much for this place, but I could pay off my debts. Obviously, it's just an idea at this stage."

"Yes, well… I'll make the tea."

"Thanks. I'll be up in a minute."

Olivia found Luke on the sofa with the TV on. He was out of school uniform and looking comfortable in a 'Death by Pollution' T-shirt.

He eyed her smart attire.

"Going somewhere?" he asked.

"Yes. Can I get you anything? Tea? Coffee?" *Poison?*

"I'm fine, thanks."

She went into the tiny kitchen and put the kettle on. While it boiled, she came back to the doorway.

"You could be a champion, you know. Instead of just being a T-shirt guy."

Luke's brow furrowed.

"Is that how you see me? A T-shirt guy?"

"Actually, I see you as an outsider. I should know. Now, how about if I tell you a story that might help us with the bridge."

"Not now, thanks."

"Luke, this is important."

"You're right. I am a T-shirt guy – an insignificant cog in the machine."

"Most people are insignificant cogs in the machine. About the bridge – I found something."

"Can this wait? I'm late for a call."

He pulled his phone out and went into the bedroom.

Not for the first time, she wondered what it must be like to have Luke for a son. Or to have a daughter like Viv's foster-care girl, Sadie. She had never thought of Jamie like that. All was calm there. But was that too idealized?

It seemed so.

Olivia regretted her behaviour towards Viv. She needed to put it right.

And Luke too.

"There's a meeting," she called through the closed door. "I want you to come along."

There was no response.

"It's not optional, Luke. I want you there."

Still there was no response.

"You cannot be T-Shirt guy forever."

*

Just after half-six, in the early evening sunshine, Olivia, Sue, Cam, and Luke were on the other side of the road to

Gus Brody Autos waiting for Ken and Beano, who were coming along from Colshot Lane.

Olivia was happily hearing all about Sue and Cam's long weekend in Brighton.

"Cam introduced me to a whole new experience," said Sue. "My tongue nearly melted…"

All eyes were on her.

"A strawberry daiquiri," she explained.

She went on to describe their calorie-laden tour of Brighton while they made their way to the village hall.

Inside, Ken exchanged greetings with a few other attendees. To Olivia's surprise, Luke joined in – talking to a woman about commuting.

For a moment, she couldn't quite recall where she'd seen her… then it came back. It was the woman who'd had her car's M.O.T. inspection at Gus's garage. Was it a teen crush? The woman had to be twice Luke's age.

She listened in on them, to make sure nothing untoward was going on. Luke spotted her and looked embarrassed, but he continued talking.

Caught red-handed, Olivia took refuge in her parish council guidance manual while she waited for the meeting to start. She settled on a page near the end of the document.

'…the Act of 2007 states that a parish council may rename itself as a 'village council', 'neighbourhood council' or 'community council'…

Interesting…

Perhaps she would suggest a change from parish council to community council just to annoy them. She looked around.

Maybe not.

Once the meeting was under way, there was no messing around. Item One was the council's intention to co-opt

Son of Colin onto its body.

Before Olivia could focus properly, the clerk was uttering the words, "If anyone here objects, please address the meeting."

Was this it? The iconic scene in a Hollywood movie, where the hero stands defiantly against the bad guys.

"No...?" said the clerk.

Olivia felt the adrenalin in her veins... her heart thumped... she stood and cleared her throat and prepared to say, "I am Spartacus!"

Instead, in the brightest voice she could muster, she said. "I object."

All eyes turned in her direction.

"I'd like to challenge it," she added. "I'll stand for election if I have to."

The clerk seemed to weigh her up. He took a moment and then prepared, quite obviously, to say something equally momentous. Just like her, he cleared his throat in order to speak loudly and clearly. It was important that the whole hall heard his history-making words.

"Who are you?" he said.

Okay, not the best launch...

"Olivia Holmes. I live at Whitman Farm in Colshot Lane."

The clerk acknowledged her and then ran through the criteria to make sure that everyone understood the situation and that valuable council time and resources weren't being abused. He also asked if anyone present knew of any grounds that might prevent an election being called. Olivia guessed that Alan Curtis-Fisher's scowl was deemed an insufficient reason.

"It's an election then," said the clerk. "Assuming the conditions are met by two or more candidates, I'm looking at early September."

For Olivia, the rest of the meeting went by in a blur. She would be fighting an election. It seemed so unlikely. She had come to Kent to find a new life – but absolutely not this one.

After the meeting, she tried to focus her thoughts.

"Ready for home?" Sue asked.

"Home? There's an election in eight weeks. We should be knocking on doors."

"No, we should go home and prepare properly."

Olivia took a breath.

"You're right. I'm being stupid."

"I'm glad you think so," said Luke. "If you knock on doors unprepared, you'll just confirm what most people think."

"Which is…?"

"That a parish council by-election is bigger news to you than it is to them,"

"Great."

"Still, it might fun using the dark arts. Machiavelli says it's okay to kill off your opponents."

"Yes, the ends justify the means – and yes, I know that isn't the exact quote. So what are we thinking publicity-wise?"

"Not sure," said Sue. "I could take photos of you meeting people. There's always an element of glad-handing and kissing babies on the campaign trail."

"Do not roll your eyes, Luke," said Olivia, but she felt a twinge in her heart at the mention of kissing babies.

"Leaflets," said Sue.

"I'll leave you to it," said Luke. "Have fun."

Fifteen minutes later, Olivia, Sue and Cam were back at Cam's, opening a bottle of rhubarb wine and discussing political finances.

"You can spend £740 plus a few pennies per registered

voter in the parish," he advised them. "So, perhaps around a thousand."

Olivia raised an eyebrow.

"That much? So, my mega-splash of fifty pounds won't break any rules."

"Fifty?" queried Sue.

"Well, I'm not made of money."

Olivia lifted her glass and took in the bouquet. What notes were these?

Raspberry, liquorice...

She took a sip.

Wowser, that's strong!

"You'll need an agent," said Cam.

"I can do that," said Sue.

"Okay," said Cam, "but if my wife-to-be is an agent, remember to fight clean and maintain the integrity of the election."

Olivia smiled.

"Does Sue go to prison if I don't?"

"Something like that. Candidates are public figures. Don't forget that anyone can take a closer look at what you're up to. Your opponents, voters, the media. Your election agent is legally responsible for your campaign's financial management."

"Sue's perfectly safe."

"Yes, of course," said Cam, "But just to be clear, things that are out: Fraud, obviously. Bribing people to vote for you. Treating, which is handing out gifts for the same reason. And please don't threaten anyone."

"I think we'll be okay," said Olivia.

"There are other things to avoid, but I'm sure they won't apply to you."

"Great," said Sue.

"Obviously, don't sign up any dead people to the

electoral role and get them to vote for you."

"Noted," said Olivia.

27

Stepping-Stone Viv

On a sizzling, sunny Tuesday afternoon, Olivia pulled up outside Viv's place. This would be it. That video was going to happen, no matter how ridiculous or embarrassing it might be. Viv was a friend — and friends had to be supported.

Getting out of the car, she waved to Viv, who was already at her front door. It occurred to Olivia that her friend's rainbow T-shirt would probably look good on camera. She hoped her plain charcoal blouse wouldn't be too dull.

"Someone looks ready for action," said Viv.

Olivia smiled.

Yes, ready for action. That's me.

"I'm sorry about leaving early last time, Viv."

"You already apologized on the phone."

"You have enough on your plate with a vineyard, a daughter, and being a foster-parent."

"It's not a prison sentence. I chose it."

"How are they – Ellie and Sadie?"

"Ellie's fine. Sadie's moved on. I'm expecting a fresh arrival tonight. A ten-year-old boy who's not having a happy time right now."

Olivia felt two inches tall in the shadow of this impressive woman.

"Tea?" Viv offered.

A moment later, they were in the kitchen, where Viv put the kettle on.

"How did you become drawn to foster-caring?" Olivia wondered.

"I was a foster child once – a long time ago."

"Oh… that's… I mean…"

What do I mean?

"When I was six, we were thrown out of our flat because my dad never paid the rent. Let's just say the local pubs did okay. He didn't see it was his fault though. He blamed my mum and me for holding him back. If it weren't for us, he could have done this or that. We ended up in some rough places. One time, the people next door sold drugs and there was usually trouble. Late night noise. Scary noise. Fights. I remember a man shouting up at the window. He didn't know it was me looking down. I can still hear him calling to someone called Debs and all the things he was going to do to her if she didn't give him money. So many years ago, but it's as vivid as ever."

"That's awful."

"I tried to rationalize it. That he wasn't really a violent man, that Debs really did owe him money. I wondered if I should pretend to be Debs and throw him my pocket money."

"Oh my God… and did you?"

"Yes, it was a few coins I'd saved. I opened the window and dropped them. I heard them clatter to the ground and then he got even angrier. I cried because it was all I had and then my mother came and closed the window. We just shook with fear for hours. I don't think I slept that night or the next few nights."

Olivia didn't understand.

"The police didn't get involved…?"

"No – and it got worse. My dad fell in with them, became a courier. Guess who got arrested when the police finally got involved?"

"Your dad?"

"He got three years in jail, did half the sentence and never came home. He said he needed a fresh start and went up North to work as a van driver for a company that accepted ex-cons."

"Did you get away from the place you were living?"

"Yes, we got another place, but it was worse."

Olivia shuddered. "I can't imagine."

"A ground floor flat that had been broken into a million times. We felt so unsafe. And there would be men knocking on the door after midnight asking for people who had lived there. I think between the ages of six and ten I went to bed permanently scared. I used to make up stories about happy families and lovely little houses in leafy streets."

"I'm not surprised. Where was this?"

"North London. In the end, my mum married to get us away to South-East London. He was the loveliest man you could hope to meet… until you spoke out of turn. He caused us a lot of pain. My mother only married him to get us to a better place. We didn't get to a better life though. When I was thirteen, I ran away from home. It's a long story but I couldn't go back."

"So, you ended up in foster-care…"

"It's a time when it's easy to feel alone, to feel that no

one's interested. Self-esteem slips away and you feel that maybe it's all your fault. Some kids feel depressed and suicidal. Others lash out."

"But you were okay… in the end."

"In the end, yes."

Olivia was touched. Who better than Viv to guide troubled teens back to a safe and worthwhile path?

Viv smiled. "Every young person deserves an opportunity to grow. My job is to make sure they know the opportunity exists. I'm not here to help them succeed in life. I wish I could arrange that for them, but I can't. I'm here to make sure they don't throw away the chance."

"And you do that by providing a home?"

"Yes, for a time I provide stability. Even as a stepping-stone, it might be enough."

Olivia liked that. Potential was everything at a young age.

She thought of Luke. Was there more she could do? Not to fix everything for him, but to keep his options alive until he was smart enough to consider what he really wanted to do.

Viv made the tea and grabbed a packet of choc chip cookies.

"Ready for the video?" she asked.

"Absolutely."

"I thought we'd do a poem."

"You mean you'll spare me the fun of singing?"

Viv smiled and led them outside to the table and chairs on the patio.

"I'll read it once through, so you know what you've let yourself in for. Then we'll record it taking a line each. So, let's be very solemn as we tell this tragic tale. Ahem…"

Olivia could only marvel as a Viv took a breath.

'A woman called Liz had a strangely full vine,
Worthy of publicity
Its beachball-sized grapes, they numbered just nine,
Such was their sheer sphericity.

With a cry that said, "it's a record load!"
She prepared like an Olympic weightlifter.
But such was the bulk of each juice-filled globe,
She conceded, "It'll be hard to shift yer!"

So heavy was the first, Liz wheezed a rude noun,
And tripped in a fruit-burst commotion.
As she writhed on the ground, three more crashed
down,
And she drowned in a very small ocean.'

Olivia laughed. It was too ridiculous for words. She also
guessed that recording it might take a few goes.

"Well, what do you think?" Viv asked.

"I think you're amazing."

"Oh… thanks. I meant what did you think of the
poem."

"Oh, we'll definitely go viral."

"Great. Ellie should be here soon. She'll film us."

They took a sip of hot tea and enjoyed a moment of
calm.

"Going back to young people for a minute…" Olivia
began.

Viv's friendly expression gave her all the room she
needed.

"I'm trying to help my partner with his son. It's not a
dangerous situation or anything, but he doesn't seem to fit
in easily."

"And what's your role?"

"That's a good question."

Olivia explained her plans to get Gus to move in with her, and Luke's arrival wrecking all that, and her desire to help sort it out in the best way – without giving up on her own wishes.

"You could be a proxy parent."

"How would I do that?"

"Aim to help Luke have some islands of stability in his life. Offer him a calm, safe space. A calm atmosphere creates a calm individual, and calm individuals make better choices – so be on hand if he needs you."

"Okay…"

"Whatever potential we have will never amount to much if we can't co-operate with anyone. Giving young people a sense of purpose in an area they love is so important if we're to encourage co-operation. They have the energy to achieve things, but they often lack direction. And sometimes there are negative influences waiting to draw them in."

"I can imagine."

"Try to understand and forgive. Don't become a doormat though. You need to boss the situation. It's finding the right way – that's the tricky part. Steer him down a path he would choose himself. That's your route to co-operation."

"I'm taking notes."

"Give him responsibilities he can handle but don't overdo the praise. Be a realist. No one should let off fireworks because their child tidied their room. Ask his opinion on things. Build self-esteem. Help him see that opportunity doesn't care who we are. Explain that it's an unstoppable universal force absolutely coming his way. Help him understand that it's really, really worth being ready for it."

"Ah, there you are," said Ellie, coming out to join them. "My leading ladies…"

28

Commitment

Olivia was attending her penultimate Level Two wine class. Next week's final class and exam wouldn't be her last excursion to the Hallam Hotel though – over the weeks, this had become an oasis of calm and sanity.

In the lobby, Spencer was on his phone. They exchanged smiles. He was such an enthusiast and had already settled on taking both the Level Three and Four courses. He wanted to become a wine professional and eventually write books on the subject. He certainly had the commitment.

Entering the classroom, she spotted Gail in conversation with Norman. Gail was now all booked for a spot of chateau-sitting in France. The option to go with her was still there, it was just that Olivia had found herself unable to say yes and unwilling to say no. Had she been subconsciously hoping Gail would grow bored with her indecision and choose someone else? Maybe, but it didn't matter. Gail seemed to be happy to leave the door open.

Olivia soon found herself talking about New Zealand whites with Alicia and Felicity, although any conclusions they might have reached were cut short by Hannah starting the class.

"Hello everyone. It's lovely to see you all for our last but one time together at Level Two. Let's start with something specific and work outward from there regarding location, environment, and other factors. Who likes Merlot?"

Most hands went up.

"Okay, so Merlot is a dark blue grape variety. The name comes from merle, the French for blackbird. It's a soft, fleshy, early ripening grape which produces a popular wine. But it also forms part of the blend used in Bordeaux wine. I'm sure we're all familiar with DNA analysis in TV cop shows."

"Yes," said Alicia, "and those genealogy sites where you pay good money to learn your ancestors were from a completely different country to the one you expected."

"I'd rather not know," said Norman. "If I've got noble blood, I'd prefer not to have any fuss made about it."

"Yes… well," said Hannah, retaking the reins, "thanks to DNA analysis moving into our chosen area of interest, we recently discovered Merlot's parentage as Cabernet Franc and Magdeleine Noire des Charentes. Now the latter was an obscure and unnamed variety until just a few years ago. But once technology declared, 'hey, you're Merlot's mother' then the grape took the name I mentioned – Magdeleine Noire des Charentes."

Olivia smiled. A mother and her child reunited. She liked that.

"So, before we try some, let's look at where Merlot came from and where it's spread to over time…"

*

After the class, Olivia was enjoying a glass of chilled Sauvignon Blanc on the patio at Whitman Farm. She felt a little guilty that it wasn't Merlot, but summer surely meant white, or perhaps rosé. She supposed that was the ultimate underlying basis for wine preference. It was possible to break everything down into specific notes and so on, but sometimes members of the wine-buying public would simply say, "I know what I like."

Aside from enjoying her wine, she was checking her notebook. Twelve months ago, they had hot weather with barely a breeze. As she'd noted, 'Still air, the hum of a bumble bee, the chirps and cheeps of small birds. This is country life. You can't hurry Mother Nature. There is no app for that.'

Maybe once again it would be a matter of getting water to the vines by hose and by canister on a wheelbarrow.

Bella came over with a slimy tennis ball wedged in her jaws.

Olivia took the drool-covered object and threw it a little way – although not so far as to get anywhere near a vine. While Bella chased after it, Olivia considered that in ten to twelve weeks she would complete a second growing season. Hopefully, Sue and Milo would be on hand to help at harvest time, even if it were just for fun. It gave her a warm glow.

Bella returned and dropped the ball at her feet. And Olivia smiled. Life at Whitman Farm was almost perfect.

Her phone pinged. It was Luke.

'I'll be staying with Beth for a bit. Dad thought I should let you know.'

Olivia didn't know how to respond. She wanted to fix everything, but she couldn't. He wouldn't be spending the summer holidays in Scotland, but how would it be during those six sunny weeks?

Maybe she wasn't good enough for this kind of situation – but she knew someone who was.

Channelling Viv, she replied.

'Keep safe and well. There's a place here if you need it. No questions asked x'

*

Later, getting ready for bed, Olivia thought about commitment.

A council member?

She couldn't quite see an election victory. Perhaps it would be better to stage a coup. She'd be a benevolent dictator. She would allow Alan Curtis-Fisher twenty-four hours to burn his 'by appointment only' sign.

From her bedroom window, she peered out over the vineyard. It was dark but she could always see it in her mind's eye. She had put in the hours, days, weeks, and months to know it by heart.

Commitment...

She'd offered that to Gus.

Was she a lightweight?

No.

Was he?

A year ago, in this house... with Leo. Happy... entwined... more empowered than ever... truly merging with country life... suggesting to her man that they take this to the next level... suggesting that they live together... and Leo leaving, driving away in his van, never to return.

Her phone pinged. It was her daily inspirational poem – but she put the phone down without reading it.

Commitment...

She didn't want to drive Gus away. Or Luke.

But she didn't want this current situation to go on either.

She climbed into bed – her thoughts tumbling from Luke and Gus to wine and France.

29

Hello, I'm Olivia Holmes

On Saturday morning, armed with leaflets, Olivia and Sue were making their way up Colshot Lane to the main road. On Thursday and Friday they had knocked on at least eighty doors to get the word out. Now, they were hoping to match that number in a single day.

"Any news on Luke?" Sue asked.

Olivia wasn't in the mood to discuss it in great detail.

"He's settling back into life with his aunt. It's just that we… well, Gus, Beth and Luke need to work out a plan."

They stopped briefly at Gus's place. He didn't have any work on so was busy cleaning the garage doors.

"So… electioneering?" he said.

"Yes," said Sue. "Today, Maybrook, tomorrow… more of Maybrook."

Gus wished them well.

A short while later, they were halfway down Southway picking up where they had left off – by a 'Land Acquired' sign that boasted of forty-eight new homes to be developed where May's Brook, coming up from the south, turned west towards its confluence with the Hanway stream a mile outside the village.

"Okay," said Olivia. "Let's be fearless."

They slipped into the nearest adjoining turning and stopped outside the first house. Ringing the bell triggered both trepidation and hope.

A moment later, an elderly woman opened the door. "Yes?"

"Hello, I'm Olivia Holmes. I'm sorry to bother you on a Saturday, but you might know we'll be having a vote soon on who takes the vacancy on the parish council. I know it's not affairs of state, but I'm very passionate about finding better ways to serve the local community…"

"No thank you," said the woman as she closed the door.

"Right…" said Olivia, refusing to feel deflated.

The next few citizens were equally disinterested in parish affairs.

"It's like we're asking them to help unblock a drain," Sue observed.

The next couple of homes provided a more cordial welcome, although neither seemed troubled about a new bridge half a mile away down Potter's Lane, which they considered outside the village.

More homes received a knock and a leaflet, with two people expressing support. Most were non-committal though, closing the door with a firm smile.

Coming back up Southway, the next turning, Dryden Way, was a long one, with at least fifty homes. Support was scant and it felt like a waste of time.

At the next turning, a pretty cul-de-sac called Lodge Way, Olivia walked straight past.

Sue looked puzzled.

"Not going in?"

"No."

But Olivia stopped.

"Actually, yes."

"Who were you hoping to avoid?"

"Old Roper."

"Ah."

Olivia knew his address – as a candidate she was entitled to a copy of the electoral roll. Of course, that still left the other homes.

At the first house, there seemed to be a fire at the back – although the man answering the door in Bermuda shorts and holding a chilled bottle of beer suggested the billowing smoke might be down to charcoal and sausages.

They tried the next house along – a large pale green bungalow set back from the road on a sizeable plot. The front garden was full of pink and white rose bushes and an old car that was clearly a classic sports model of some kind.

It made Olivia smile to think she was getting her campaign going before Old Roper was aware of it.

She rang the doorbell.

It took a moment before there was any noticeable activity, and then a middle-aged woman materialized behind the frosted glass to open the door.

"Hello, I'm Olivia Holmes..."

"Who?"

"Olivia Holmes. I'm sorry to bother you on a Saturday, but you probably know we'll soon be having a vote on who takes the vacancy on the parish council. I know it's not affairs of state, but I'm very passionate about finding ways to better serve the local community."

"One moment."

The woman disappeared back inside. She returned a couple of minutes later and took a good long look at Olivia's face.

"Yes so," said Olivia, "we have some serious issues to deal with. There's the new bridge over the Hanway for one thing. As I say, it's a serious business and I want to assure you that I'm a serious person."

The woman held up an iPad. A familiar video was playing.

"Is this you?"

The woman unmuted it so they could both hear a poem about oversized grapes.

"Yes," said Olivia. "That's me."

The woman shook her head slowly and closed the door.

Olivia's phone pinged.

It was a text from Gail.

'Champagne trip off. Stand by for news.'

Olivia struggled to process the information.

"Lunch?" Sue suggested.

Olivia checked her watch. It was just before one o'clock.

"Why not."

*

The Royal Standard was reasonably busy when they arrived. In one corner, Ken was with Ted and Tom discussing dentures, while in another, Alan Curtis-Fisher was with Old Roper and a couple of their friends.

"Election leaflets?" Alan Curtis-Fisher asked.

Olivia realized she was still clutching a batch. She put them in her bag and tried to ignore the man she hoped to be serving alongside come September. She focused instead on ordering lunch for her and Sue at the bar – where Gus was having a sandwich. She didn't get involved beyond a quick hello as he'd teamed up with a couple of guys who were watching a pre-season football match on TV. Olivia wasn't sure who was playing but got the impression it was an English team on tour in South-East Asia. It seemed a substitute was coming on.

"Not interrupting, am I?"

"No, of course not," said Gus. He gave her a peck on the cheek.

Olivia wondered. "Are substitutes not as good as those who start the game?"

"Depends," said one of the men with Gus. "This one's a waste of space."

Olivia gave up on football. She also decided not to mention the France trip being taken off the agenda. In fact, she would wait until she'd seen Gail in person to find out what had gone wrong.

"We'll eat outside," she advised Annie once she'd ordered.

She and Sue took their spritzers into the beer garden and found a table. The large yellow umbrella sheltered them from the sun, but there was nothing to shelter them from Alan Curtis-Fisher and Old Roper who had followed them outside.

"The future of the village is at stake," said Old Roper.

Olivia scoffed. "It's Maybrook, not Game of Thrones."

"We can't have people throwing their weight around, especially those who are only here because they got a free vineyard."

"That's a little unfair," Sue insisted.

"Ignore them," said Olivia.

Old Roper eyed his master. "If it wasn't for her great aunt, she'd have no idea if Maybrook was in Kent or Kentucky."

Olivia let that one go, as it was true.

Unexpectedly, Alan Curtis-Fisher handed her a professionally produced handout. It was headed: The

Maybrook Society.

She looked closer and sighed a little before passing it to Sue.

"Oh, you're in the photo," said her cousin.

"It's me and Son of Colin at an informal get-together."

"It doesn't look very informal. Well, apart from you."

Sue read the words below to herself and then looked up.

"Is this what's meant by the dark arts?"

Olivia took it back at read the text below the photo.

'Two great candidates for the parish council. Local businessman Jason Brunton, son of much-loved Colin…" Olivia skipped over the short eulogy. "…and Olivia Holmes, fresh down from London to take over her inheritance of a vineyard. How the other half lives! The Society is supporting Jason, but it's important that you make your own choice.'

Alan Curtis-Fisher and Old Roper went back inside, no doubt congratulating themselves on a good start to their campaign.

Olivia puffed out her cheeks.

"If Luke were here, he'd quote Machiavelli. It's okay to kill your enemies. The ends justify the means – or words to that effect."

Her phone pinged. It was a text from an unrecognized number.

'What is your policy on bench repairs?' It went on to give some details and was signed 'Connie'.

She'd had a few of these now – the price of putting her phone number on her flyers. People had asked:

'What are your policies on new homes for local people?'

'What are your thoughts on electric car charging points?'

'Will we have Christmas decorations on the High Street

this year?'

She showed them to Sue.

"I can help you with those. I'll have a word with Cam. We can give some professional-sounding replies. No bother at all."

"Thanks."

"I reckon we can get a few more house calls done than we thought. What do you think?"

"I'm wondering if it's worth it."

"Of course it's worth it. We agreed – identify supportive households and build a rapport over the next few weeks."

Olivia nodded.

"Yes… of course. We'll do that."

30

Sink or Swim

Reaching the Hallam Hotel on a warm Wednesday evening, Olivia pulled into a parking space, switched off the engine and took a moment. She should have been thinking of young wines. At least, that's what the notes for this evening's class suggested. It was especially important as this was the final class at Level Two with an exam at the end of it.

She felt a twinge of nerves.

No, she would be fine.

Young wine, young wine…

According to Hannah, young red wines tended to assault the palate. But Olivia would be professional. Assess the hue – the bluer, the younger. Take in the aroma – is the character clean and fresh? Is the fruit detectable? Are there secondary aromas? Dark fruit and spice in the Pinot Noir? Cassis in the cabernet? And tasting? Are the tannins green or ripe? Do they rudely storm the tastebuds or arrive in style? And what about the finish? Is there one worth mentioning?

Thankfully, the day before, there had been no such qualms about Whitman Farm's sparkling. A final tasting of the first batch went perfectly. Toasting Sue and Cam at their wedding was now definitely on.

In the hotel lobby, Spencer and Alicia were discussing vineyard getaways. Olivia dodged them and made for Gail in the main room. Gail though was deep in a private conversation with Hannah.

Norman was free though.

"Did you decide about Level Three?" he asked.

"Oh… yes, I'm in."

"Just think – we'll be together for sixteen Tuesday evenings."

"I can't wait."

But Olivia's mind was on France. She wanted to go.

"Hi," said Spencer, joining them. "Ever thought of offering vineyard breaks at your place?"

Olivia shook her head.

"I don't think I'd have the patience for endless guests coming and going."

Spencer smiled warmly.

"So… about now, you're doing what?"

"Turning untidy rows into a neatly manicured vista."

"I prefer the natural look," said Norman.

Olivia wasn't in the mood to give a lecture, but in Norman's case she was prepared to make an exception.

"The canopy of leaves and has to be managed to get as much sunlight on the grapes as possible. Fruit in the shade doesn't do much. Also, too many leaves create moist conditions for mildew."

"Couldn't you just pick off the rotten grapes?" said Norman.

Good grief…

Gail joined them.

Ah!

"So… Gail…?"

"Sorry about that. I've got a chance to go to Canada. I can't miss out."

"Oh wow. Great. I hear Canada's amazing."

"Yes."

"So that's it regarding France?"

"Not necessarily," said Gail. "For you, I mean."

"Um…?" Olivia wasn't quite with her.

"The whole thing was booked in your name."

"My name…?" Olivia still didn't get it.

"This friend of a friend… she only agreed to put my name at the top of her list when I explained I'd be going with an English vineyard owner."

The penny dropped.

"I see."

Gail smiled. "Would you be interested in Provence?"

"Provence? What for?"

"There's a house-sitting vacancy come up on their network. I know it's way off your region of choice."

"It is a bit. I don't know anything about Provence."

"You don't need to. You just have to enjoy the wine and talk to the workforce about their processes."

"I know a bit," said Spencer. "Rosé is big. And I speak reasonable French."

"Brilliant," said Gail.

"Well, that's fantastic," said Spencer. "I'd be happy to take Gail's place. You're doubly determined to go, Olivia. So am I."

Olivia forced her eyes not to widen. It would be an educational trip. She'd only be going in order to deepen her knowledge of wine.

"I'll send you the details," said Gail.

"Could I have your attention, please?" It was Hannah with an older man who had come in without Olivia noticing. "Let me introduce Terry. He runs our Level Three course which starts in October."

"Hello everyone," said Terry, his voice as smooth and rounded as a Ruby port, "I'm Terry Cartwright. I do hope we'll see you all again soon. Our Level Three classes run on Tuesday evenings in this very room. It would be a real pleasure to see you all taking your wine knowledge a step closer to a professional standard, and I can promise it's a wonderful journey worthy of your time."

Olivia warmed to him. He was like a much-loved uncle from the movies.

Terry went on to tell them a little more about what they could expect before handing back to Hannah. He departed with a cheery wave.

"Okay," said Hannah, "today we'll look at young wines. We'll start by looking at how winemaking and bottle ageing influence the style and quality of wine and…"

"Is that red *and* white?" asked Norman.

"Mainly red."

The shorter class flashed by, finishing fifty minutes ahead of their usual time. Hannah then arranged them around the room to take the multiple-choice exam that had no doubt been on most people's minds all evening.

"Confident?" Spencer asked.

"Yes," said Olivia, half-wondering if he was referring to the exam or potentially spending time with him in the hot, romantic South of France. "Well, mainly yes."

"Now please relax," said Hannah as she began to place the exam papers face down in front of them. "You might be nervous at first, but once you hit your stride, there'll be no stopping you."

Olivia flashed a glance at Spencer.

That's what worries me.

"Now remember," Hannah continued, "there aren't any trick questions. It's strictly limited to what we've learned over the past eight weeks."

Olivia took a breath and attempted to calm her nerves. *It's just an exam… that's all.*

A few moments later, they were ready.

"Right, so you have forty-five minutes. Please turn your papers over. Good luck."

Olivia turned the heft of stapled sheets over and braced herself.

Hard or easy?

She studied the first question.

1. Choose the two parent grapes of Cabernet Sauvignon.
a) Grenache
b) Cabernet Franc
c) Sauvignon Blanc
d) Pinot Noir
e) Magdeleine Noire des Charentes

Olivia's racing pulse slowed. At least she wouldn't score zero.

She placed a neat X against 'Cabernet Franc' and one against 'Sauvignon Blanc'.

She moved on to the next question.

2. Choose the two parent grapes of Merlot.
a) Grenache
b) Cabernet Franc
c) Sauvignon Blanc
d) Pinot Noir
e) Magdeleine Noire des Charentes

She chose with confidence: 'Cabernet Franc' and 'Magdeleine Noire des Charentes'. She knew that Merlot and Cabernet Sauvignon were half-siblings.

3. Which grape do we associate with blanc de blancs Champagne?

She didn't need to study the options to know it was Chardonnay.

She was pleased.

This might not end in disaster…

*

After the class, everyone fell into a round of relieved chatter. It seemed that all were confident of at least some level of success. Farewells were then said to those who wouldn't be taking the Level Three classes.

"France is going to be absolutely amazing," said Spencer. "Two budding wine professionals building their reputations."

It didn't seem to leave any room for a challenge, and before she could properly consider what she actually thought and wanted, he was away with Hannah and three others in a taxi to have dinner in Ashford.

On the drive home, Olivia considered how it would be in France, on a vineyard in the Provence region – Spencer searching for the one, glasses of chilled rosé being consumed, a beautiful sunset, peace, quiet, and her wishing her 'one' would get his act together.

What exactly *would* happen?

It was a lot to think about. Grapes, wine, exam results, Gus, Spencer, France. And, as she pulled up outside Whitman Farm, there was Luke to think about too – he was standing on the doorstep weighed down by a battered red rucksack.

31

Luke and Alice

Olivia thought of making tea or coffee and asking Luke what was going on. But this was his first visit to Whitman Farm, so once he'd dumped his rucksack and freshened up, she led him out to the vines.

"What do you think?" she asked.

"It's great. Dad says you work hard."

"I got lucky, but yes, I started working hard to make something of the opportunity."

"*Carpe diem* – didn't you say that once?"

Luke ruffled Bella's fur. Olivia smiled.

That's a first.

"It's a good job I didn't stay out," she mused. "You might have been on the doorstep all evening."

"No, another twenty minutes and I'd have given up."

"Right… well, I'm glad I got back in time."

She paused at a vine and tucked a wayward strand back into place.

"I saw your poem," he said.

"On YouTube?"

"Yes, Dad mentioned it." There was no hint of mirth or mockery. "Are you a fan of poetry?"

They walked on.

"Kind of… I had an inspirational daily poem thing on my phone, but I deleted it. I'm trying to draw my inspiration from the life I have. This place, my family, friends, Gus… you, perhaps."

"You've only known me six weeks."

"Seven."

They paused again and Luke made a superficial attempt to examine a vine.

"You asked me about the future," he said.

"Just to be clear, you're not about to turn sarcastic or anything?"

"When I was younger…"

"Younger? You're fifteen."

"When I was younger, the future was something I could leave to other people. My mother, for example."

"Oh, Luke…"

"Then, not long ago, I looked up and there it was, like a giant asteroid heading for Earth. Trying to revise for the mock-exams made it worse."

"Exams can be stressful, but we get through them."

"Oh? When was the last time you sat an exam?"

"An hour ago."

Luke looked confused, so Olivia helped him out.

"It was the final night at wine class – followed by an exam."

"Ah right. Sorry. How did you get on?"

"Okay, I think – but we're talking about you."

"Yes, well… it's not so much the exams. It's more what they represent. The end of avoidance. People ask me what I'm going to do when I leave school. Will I go to university? What will I study? What career will I go for? Between you and me, I haven't a clue."

"That's not a crime."

"No really, I feel I should have an idea. I'm meant to be the smart kid with all the answers."

"Nobody has all the answers. We just do the best we can. And when there's someone offering good advice, we listen. We might not always take it, but we grow to learn who we can rely on. We might even get that wrong too, by the way."

"Is this a pep talk your mum gave you?"

"No… no, it's not."

"Your dad?"

"No…"

"Do you still see your parents?"

"No, they've both passed on."

"Ah, sorry. Dad never said."

"No need to be sorry. It was a long time ago."

"What did they do?"

"Workwise? Mum was a National Health Service cleaner and Dad ran a used car business."

"Cars? A bit like Dad."

"I suppose. It was a tough time though."

"Dad's having a tough time too."

"Yes, well, my dad… he took his own life when it got too much."

"Oh… wow. That is not good."

"No… he tried his best, but there was a recession and the debts gradually got to him. It was all collapsing… his life's work… he couldn't take the failure."

Luke seemed a little shaken, so Olivia changed the focus.

"Hungry?"

Twenty minutes later, they were seated on the patio,

munching on the remaining emergency pizza.

"Last day of term on Friday," she said. "Do you all sing School's Out?"

"I'm sure one or two will."

"Six whole weeks of summer…" Olivia reflected on her own memories of that tantalising prospect always coming around too slowly and disappearing too fast.

Luke looked up from his pizza.

"Something you said a while back… about me doing music, art, poetry, theatre. You said it was interesting."

"It is."

"You said we should do the things we enjoy to the best of our ability."

"Yes."

"I think you also mentioned something about me taming my ego, but we can skip over that."

Olivia smiled.

Luke went on, "I liked what you said, only it took a while to sink in. But it's not just about doing the things we enjoy. We can stretch it to doing the things we care about."

"Yes, the things we're passionate about, the things that make us feel worthwhile. I remember being young and facing a bunch of useless career choices… choices I had to consider because they were all that was available to me."

"You did okay though. In the end."

"I got lucky, remember? That can never be the plan."

"No…"

"Can I tell you about Alice?" Olivia summoned the musicians' photo on her phone and pointed her out. "She passed away a long time ago, but had she lived, she would have been a couple of years younger than Sue. I think she would have been a partner in the vineyard."

She handed Luke the phone for him to have a closer look.

"I wonder what they were playing?" he said.

Olivia gave it some thought.

"Mozart, Beethoven… or maybe they were a classical version of Folkie-Karaoke. Oasis played as Brahms."

Luke considered it.

"Dad got me playing flute when I was young."

"Did he? I never knew."

"I expect Alice was better than me."

"Oh… that's…"

"Fliss Fairfax taught me. She taught Dad too."

"Flute and violin?"

"She taught four or five instruments."

Luke studied the photo again.

"Did Alice live here?"

"No, but somehow I feel she belonged here."

"I'm not sure I belong in Maybrook," he said, handing the phone back. "It might be nice to belong somewhere though."

"You'll be fine," said Olivia, putting the phone away. "You'll find the place for you."

"How about you? Will you go back to London?"

Olivia was stumped.

"London?"

"When you've done a few years here."

"I'm never going back to London. Is that what you think?"

Luke looked a little uncertain.

"Maybe."

Something dawned on Olivia. Did a boy with no real sense of home believe she would ever…?

"I'm not planning to team up with your dad and move to London with him, okay."

"Right. Understood."

Oh God, he thought…

194

"I'm staying, Luke. I'm not leaving Maybrook."

"Right."

"Is that helpful? Or…?"

"I'm thinking of switching schools after next year," he said. "There's a better sixth form the other side of Maidstone. The thing is… Aunt Beth's looking to remarry and move to East Sussex… and Dad and you…"

"I know. It's a lot to deal with."

Olivia thought of Viv and her foster care charges. Troubled teens. Luke wasn't all that difficult, but he was fifteen and the world hadn't exactly offered him any kind of certainty.

"So, the old stone bridge?" he said. "Is that something I should get properly involved in?"

"It might be."

"I was reading recently that people—"

"Sometimes you have to stop reading and go out and do something yourself."

"I wouldn't make a good ally."

"You don't know that."

"Most times, if I see a way to fix things, I keep it to myself. I'm not proud of it, but if others fail, then I won't be the one in the spotlight."

"That's quite a downward spiral."

"Yes, well… as I said, I'm not proud."

"This sixth form the other side of Maidstone. Is it really a better school or just a chance for a fresh start?"

"It's a fresh start. I'm hoping I can reboot everything and try again."

"You've got a whole school year and exams before you need to choose a sixth form, but it's a great idea to be thinking about it. Can I suggest something – that, in the meantime, you try to spend time with positive people, think positively, make friendships, be there for others…and on the flipside, stay away from negative, moaning gossipmongers."

"I suppose… although it's worse than you think."

"Oh?"

"I got dumped."

Olivia almost laughed but stopped herself.

Luke smiled a little.

"I think the final straw was when I described her hair as luminously glistening instead of shiny. I like words so I tend to overreach for better ones."

"You don't say."

"I'm aware of the power of simplicity, but…"

"Dark forces put temptation in your way?"

"Something like that."

"You're exploring the world, that's all. If a handy, practical young person found a shed full of amazing tools, they wouldn't limit themselves to a basic screwdriver. They'd try all kinds of things out and probably make a complete mess of whatever they were hoping to achieve. But they'd learn so much."

"I suppose so."

"See, I'm not as dim as I look."

"Exploration not ego. It's a thought."

"Too late to save the love of your life though."

"Yes."

Olivia sighed.

"We've all felt love's first bitter sting."

"But then we grow older and wiser and appreciate true love?"

"Not always. But yes, sometimes."

"We don't drag it around with us?"

"No."

"Or turn violent?"

"Certainly not!"

"Only Dad told me you threw a pizza, eggs and flour at your ex."

Gus…!

"Those were special circumstances." She didn't want to go into the business of her ex becoming a father. "Breaking up doesn't hurt forever – but sometimes it can feel like it."

"Did you make bad decisions at fifteen?"

"Yes."

"Could I sleep on your sofa tonight?"

"Luke, I have two spare bedrooms. I'll make you up a bed."

"Only if it's not too much trouble."

My darling boy…

"It is *not* too much trouble. I'd be delighted to have you stay over. There was a time I wanted to submit your name for the first manned rocket to Mars, but…"

But I'm beginning to think of you as…

"I'll text Dad," said Luke, reaching for his phone.

Twenty minutes later, back in the house while Olivia was sorting out some bedding, Gus texted her.

'Olivia Holmes, thank you for everything you're doing xxx'

Then an email came through.

It was from Hannah.

'Congratulations! 93% pass with distinction. I really hope we see you again in October for Terry's Level Three classes!'

32

Hostiles & Possibles

Saturday morning was too hot for Sue to go campaigning, so Olivia's new lodger accompanied her to the homes sprinkled in little enclaves west of the church. Luke had a definite spring in his step, although Olivia accepted that might have been down to him finishing school for the summer on the Friday.

The twentieth door they knocked produced a middle-aged woman with a paint brush in her hand.

"I'm a little busy," she said. "Is it important?"

Olivia ran through her objectives with a smile that was beginning to cause cheek-ache.

"Hmm," said the woman. "The thing is… my sister's looking to rent at Forest Edge, so we'd prefer to have car access. It's a bloody long way round otherwise."

Olivia thanked her and withdrew.

"It's not easy trying to beat Son of Colin's combination of tradition and a new bridge."

The next few calls were people they could chalk up as

'possibles'. Then they hit a run of 'no thank yous' and a 'hostile'.

"Let me try the next one," said Luke.

Olivia was relieved. Just then, her phone pinged. It was a text from Gus.

'Closing the garage lunchtime. Pub sandwich at one?'

She texted back. 'See you there.'

Meanwhile, Luke rang the bell at the next house. A moment later, an attractive woman of around thirty answered. While Luke launched into an explanatory speech, Olivia didn't need to think where she'd seen this woman before.

Luke touched on local policies concerning traffic and the bridge, but also ventured into the idea of working from a local hub as an antidote to the headache of commuting between Maybrook and London.

Olivia merged herself into the conversation by agreeing that it was a long drive to Maybrook's nearest station before turning matters back to the business of the old bridge at the end of Potter's Lane.

The woman – Abi – agreed to vote for Olivia and wished them luck.

Back on the trail, the candidate eyed her helper.

"Strange you should take over at exactly that house."

"How do you mean?"

"Have you taken a liking to her?"

"I knew she lived there. Her address is in Dad's database. And before you think it's anything weird, you're wrong."

*

Just after one o'clock, they were seated in the Royal Standard beer garden with Gus, waiting for Annie to bring out their sandwiches. Ken was with his old friend Ted at the next table discussing champagne, while Beano snoozed under the table.

Olivia couldn't help but listen in on a discussion on Dom Perignon while she sipped her drink.

"I didn't know monks were allowed to drink," said Ted.

"I'm not one for ecclesiastical regulations," said Ken, "especially 17th Century Benedictine rules. All I'm saying is Dom Perignon spent half a century in an abbey perfecting the art of making sparkling wine, which we now call Champagne thanks to him being located there. Had the Champagne region been called Cobblers then, today, people in restaurants would be snapping their fingers at the wine waiter and asking for a bottle of Cobblers."

"I've been thinking about the future," said Luke, drawing Olivia's attention back to their table.

"That makes me worry," said Gus. "Twenty years from now, you'll be making all the big decisions."

"I won't cut your pension, if that's what's bothering you."

"What have you been thinking?" Olivia asked.

And in that moment, she felt yet again that she wanted to bring Gus, Luke and herself together. In fact, that was all she really cared about – far more than any bridge or a seat on a parish council.

"University," said Luke.

Ken and Ted rose from the adjoining table.

"We're off," Ken informed them.

Beano still looked half-asleep but wagged his tail when Olivia stroked him.

"Before I go…" said Ken. He leaned closer to Olivia. "I've been thinking about a little idea that might appeal to you."

"It's not about the bridge, is it?"

"No, it's about vineyards. My knowledge of business is quite limited, but it occurred to me you might look into forming a collective with other small, local growers."

Olivia wasn't sure how to respond.

"There's already an association, Ken."

"Yes, it's a big one too, isn't it – the whole of south-east England with a committee of elected members... in fact, there are elections quite soon..."

"Really, I'm not looking to fight another election campaign."

"Yes, well, aside from all that, I was thinking about a collective of small, local vineyards that might boost your muscle in the local market. You know – a local wine of the week at local supermarkets. With five or six vineyards getting involved you'd be able to share a brand and keep up a steady supply. From what I hear, it's the supply that causes issues. That's what you have to overcome."

She thought of her own output, and that of Viv. There would be others in similar positions locally.

"I'll think about it, Ken. It's certainly an idea."

Ken and Beano departed along with Ted, who was already making noises about heading home for an afternoon nap.

Luke, meanwhile, popped to the Gents.

"Sounds interesting," said Gus. "I wonder if they do that kind of thing in France? You and your friend could find out what's what."

"Yes... unless you'd rather come with me?"

"No, not me." He spent a minute or two detailing how receipts were down and bills were up before returning to Olivia's wine pilgrimage. "You and Gail go. I can see you two... business minded during the day, then, after a couple of bottles of the local stuff..."

Olivia wasn't about to lie to Gus. Nor would she let an

omission do any damage either.

"Gail pulled out. A guy named Spencer is standing in."

"Oh."

"He's a serious wine nut, so it's strictly work. There won't be any silly stuff."

"Right. Well, as you say, it's business. It's important."

"There's a change of destination too. It's now the south of France."

"Right, well… that sounds fantastic."

"Gus? You do trust me?"

"Of course."

Olivia felt awkward, which seemed wrong.

"Luke says you had the same music teacher," she said, changing the subject.

Gus brightened.

"Fliss Fairfax. A local legend. She used to give me a Quality Street chocolate if I applied myself."

"Hmm, that's how I train Bella."

"She's a lovely old thing. I still look after her car. Free of charge, obviously."

"She's local?"

"She lives in Ralston. She's got a Honda now, but when I was a kid, she used to drive this old Morris Minor with a really whiny engine."

Olivia smiled – but her thoughts moved on from Fliss Fairfax to the conversation to come between father and son. 'Luke, I'd like you to live with me and my solid, dependable partner – when she gets back from France with some guy called Spencer.'

*

A couple of hours after lunch, Olivia and Luke were finishing their campaigning for the day, and for the week.

Olivia's plan was to avoid being a nuisance. She would return in a couple of weeks to work on those who had joined her list of 'possibles'. Those who professed support would be contacted again much nearer election day.

As for France – she wanted to go. It would be wrong to cancel it or go alone. She would see Spencer at the Level Three classes, where everyone would be aware that she hadn't trusted him to behave on a short trip. That wasn't fair. He was a would-be wine professional who would travel extensively and wouldn't be helped with a potential 'no smoke without fire' tag blighting his reputation. As Gus was quick to point out, people liked to gossip.

No, she had to go with Spencer. The only valid substitute would be Gus, as everyone would understand her making it a romantic getaway with her man. But Gus was ten thousand in debt and losing more each month. And he was too proud to be bailed out. He already owed her close to a thousand and so a charity-paid trip was out of the question. Besides, wine wasn't really his thing. Spencer was ready, willing, and able. And he was a wine nut. The only thing stopping her was the potential for a lapse – which wouldn't happen. Although she couldn't help but think back to those weekend trips with her old firm, Prior Grove. Lapses were the one thing some people looked forward to.

Undoubtedly, it was time to email Hannah and ask her to pass on a message to Spencer.

"Do you think you'll win?" Luke asked as they made their way home.

"I do. It's just… well, I still feel like an outsider poking my nose in. I also feel we need to watch out for Son of Colin. His backers won't be short of a few more tricks."

"Machiavelli?"

"I'd rather leave the dark arts to one side."

"We could get all the council members drunk."

"What a horrible thought."

"You could take photos and blackmail them into switching their support."

"Blackmail… maybe."

"Really?"

"No, of course not. Anyway, we'd never get all of them together in one place where they're not in control."

"Apart from Sue and Cam's wedding," said Luke matter-of-factly.

Olivia considered it. Cam was undoubtedly a popular former council member. They would all be there.

Reaching Gus's place, Luke opted to spend a little time with his dad. Olivia was invited to join them, but she wanted some time to think.

Back at home, she collected Bella. A good walk would clear her mind.

They stopped at Ken's place. Not just for Bella to say hello and gulp down a treat. Ken had been furtive and unhelpful over Alice, leaving her to find out what she could for herself. But that wouldn't break their friendship. Olivia wanted to let him know she'd be taking his wine collective idea seriously.

At his door though, Bella began whining.

"What is it?"

Now she could hear Beano on the other side of the door, also whining.

Olivia went to the window. Ken was inside, on the floor. Her heart thumped. Her skin suddenly felt clammy. She gasped for breath.

"Ken…?" She rapped on the glass. "Ken!"

She pulled out her phone to call the emergency services while hurrying home to grab Ken's spare keys.

33

Confessions

As the ambulance drove off, Olivia stood in Ken's doorway. Sue and Cam were just outside looking worried. Ken had been conscious but not looking good at all when they took him.

"Well," said Olivia, "I'd better check doors and windows and lock up."

"Do you want to come over for some tea or coffee?" Sue asked.

"Or wine?" said Cam.

"No, I'll head over to the hospital. See if I can find out a bit more."

Back inside the house, she closed a couple of windows and made sure the back door was locked. In the kitchen, she spotted a penknife on the worktop.

She opened it.

A memory crept up on her. A man with a penknife that turned into a corkscrew opened a bottle of white wine and passed it to Olivia's dad. He sniffed the bottle, as did

Olivia's mum. Olivia got involved too, sniffing the open neck. The wine's bouquet reminded her of…

Sweaty armpits.

Someone called the name Alice. She looked across the pub to see a young woman with pink streaks in her hair. The call had come from the man with the penknife-corkscrew.

She considered Luke and Ken. Both ends of life. But wasn't Ken once a young lad who began a new life in Maybrook?

She refocused on the here and now, and hurried home to get her car keys. Moments later, she was in the car.

"Deep breaths…"

She knew it was coming. If not today… he wouldn't be around forever.

She glanced at a text from a couple of minutes earlier.

'What is your policy on a) Litter bins and b) Public seats?'

She couldn't respond – she'd had enough.

A wine collective – yes.

The parish council?

She didn't have a policy on litter bins or public seating. She would quit the race. It had never been about joining the council. It was about becoming a part of the community. And that took time.

She started the car and pulled away.

Ten miles and a thousand thoughts later, she pulled into a hospital parking space without appreciating the glorious late afternoon sunshine.

At the Accident & Emergency reception desk, she enquired after Ken and asked the question she'd been dreading.

"How is he?"

"Are you family?" the receptionist asked.

"No."

"He's being assessed in triage at the moment," said the receptionist.

Olivia felt a surge of relief.

"Can I see him?"

"Not while he's being assessed."

"Right... fine. Thank you."

Olivia wasn't sure what to do. She went outside to take in some fresh air. And she pondered. And then she decided.

Look confident.

By the door, she observed. Then, when the receptionist was busy with someone, she breezed straight through to the triage area and began searching for her friend.

"Can I help?" asked a passing nurse.

"I'm looking for my dad."

She gave Ken's details and was shown to a side room.

Olivia hesitated at the door, and then entered. Ken was linked to a monitor. He was asleep but things were flashing and there were numbers. A good sign. Olivia's heart was so busy thumping, she wondered if they might hook her up to the machine as well.

She placed a chair by the bed and waited.

Two hours later, following a number of assessments, Ken was moved to a ward. That was good – he wasn't expected to leave them just yet.

It was Olivia who was invited to leave – the patient required rest. She insisted on staying just a little longer to help him settle in.

Suddenly Ken woke up.

"My legs gave way," he said to both her and the nurse getting him comfortable.

Olivia was grateful to hear his voice.

He gathered his breath and went on, "It's never

happened before."

"You need to rest," said the nurse.

"Exactly," said Olivia.

"They might put me in a home," said Ken.

Olivia shook her head.

"I don't think anyone's talking about homes, Ken."

The nurse wished him well and advised Olivia it was time to go. She smiled politely and promised to be no more than a couple of minutes.

"I can't live in a home," said Ken. "I've visited friends in places like that. Do you know they have the television on all day in the communal lounge? Not a second of your own time for thinking. Unless you stay in your room. But who wants to spend all day in a small room?"

"I'm sure lots of homes are wonderful, but you're getting ahead of yourself."

"But what if I'm right?"

"Then… I'd come and visit you. We'd go to the pub for lunch. Or you could come back to the vineyard with me. We could talk about the great champagnes. And we could taste them. Well, some of them."

"How's the campaign coming along?"

"Are you sure you should be talking, Ken. You had quite a turn."

"I feel a little better, thanks. And I'd like to take my mind off this place. So, the campaign…?"

"It's over. I've had enough."

"Giving up? That's not like you."

"I don't know. This time… I've done things for the wrong reason. And I'm sorry about Alice. I've been far too nosy."

Ken thought for a moment.

"Can you imagine keeping someone alive in your thoughts?" he said. "Talking to them. Asking their opinion on things?"

"Yes… I can. But I've been a pain. I won't bring it up again. We're going to be friends, Ken. Even better friends than before."

"A while ago you mentioned fate and fortune."

"Yes, I remember."

"Well… someone had to die for you to be so lucky."

Oh Alice.

"Ken, I…"

"I was against you and your cousins taking over the vineyard."

"Right." Olivia homed in on the obvious. "I'm guessing Alice was meant to inherit the vineyard."

Ken shifted his position slightly to get more comfortable.

"Yes," he said.

"But you agreed to help us."

"Thirty years had passed. There was no reason to be unhelpful other than pure pig-headedness."

"So, you started giving us the occasional tip."

"Yes, but then something unexpected happened. Sue and Milo did their bit, but you stood out. I came to respect you. What I saw you putting in… you deserved only my best efforts."

"We've always been grateful."

"She was training to be an accountant. Worked in an office. But she came alive among the vines. You'd understand that more than most."

"All too well, Ken. So, you and Gloria…?"

"Charlie wasn't best pleased."

"I dare say he wasn't."

"You have to remember it was 1962/63. The village wasn't as forward thinking as it is today. There were family pressures, society pressures… Gloria chose Charlie against all her instincts."

"Right."

"Charlie once confided in me that Gloria couldn't have children. Some kind of inner workings problem. I think he was devastated to find out it had been him all along. I mean furious about everything, obviously, but devastated too, as if one disaster wasn't enough for him."

Olivia nodded.

"So, Gloria's cousin…?"

"She stepped in. Married, no children. It's not a unique story. Thousands of people went through the same sort of thing. It was the end of the old era. Within a few years, the Beatles had long hair, girls went on the pill… but this was before all that. Back then, we lived as if 1962 were 1922. Britain was very stuffy."

"So, Gloria gave Alice away."

For Olivia, it was beyond imagining. She lost Jamie. It was hard to find any sympathy, even if Maybrook was practically Victorian back then.

"Don't judge her too harshly," said Ken. "Charlie wouldn't go along with claiming Alice as his own. He made that clear from the outset. At least Gloria gave her the chance of a life in a loving family. Try to remember that."

Olivia nodded. It wasn't easy, but she accepted that Gloria had faced some difficulties.

"So, you and Gloria living together wasn't an option…?"

Ken shook his head.

"Gloria chose to stick to her marriage vows. She was classy like that. She blamed herself for a moment of weakness and said she wouldn't cause upheaval because of it. I told her I loved her, but she asked me to keep a respectful distance – which I did."

"The quiet countryside where nothing ever happens,

eh?"

"Yes."

"Do you think she loved you?"

"If I'm honest… no."

"Ah."

"It was unfinished business from when we were young. Too much drink, perhaps. If she loved me, she would have made it known after Charlie passed away. But the fact is she never loved anyone. Poor woman."

Olivia thought of Raymond's love letter tucked behind Gloria's photo.

"So, Alice… you must have been very proud of her."

"Yes."

"Did she know you were her dad?"

"No."

"No?"

"Gloria didn't want any more complications. When Alice was eighteen, she found out who her real mother was. She was angry at first, but the situation eventually resolved itself. Gloria told her it was a happy, lovely mistake that shouldn't have happened, and that Alice should love and cherish her adoptive parents and not fret over a man who played no role in her life."

"That must have been painful."

"It was – and yet I got to know her a little from a distance. I was able to help a little too, without anyone knowing. No fanfares, just the odd anonymous contribution."

"Oh, what a tangled web we weave."

"Indeed."

"It's what Luke would say if he were here. He likes using quotes."

"So I've discovered."

"Still, you can't go wrong with a bit of Shakespeare."

"It's Walter Scott."

"Ah right."

Ken adjusted his position in the bed once again.

"You and Luke seem to be getting on better."

"Yes, we are. He's capable, but he needs to be guided a little. Is that how you saw me?"

"Not at first. But then I saw you in action. It took a while, but I started to care. Then I started to realise that fate had given me a chance to see how it might have been with Alice taking over."

"That's quite a role you gave me there, Ken. I'm glad I didn't know anything about it."

"Had my daughter handled the ups and downs as well as you, I would have been very proud."

Olivia felt the warmth in his words.

"Is that why you've always looked out for me and told me more than you tell other people?"

"Definitely."

Olivia smiled. And everything was clear. While she saw Luke as a possible, slightly distanced surrogate son, she'd never once looked in the other direction, where Ken had spent much longer seeing her as a possible, slightly distanced surrogate daughter. Unexpectedly, time slowed. For Olivia, it was like Niagara Falls coming to a halt, frozen in a single suspended moment. Then the memories of all the imagined things she had done with Jamie burst into her mind like fireworks.

It took another few moments for things to calm down, and for her to know her next move.

"I lost someone a long time ago," she uttered.

"Oh?"

She swallowed.

"You asked me if I could imagine keeping someone alive in my thoughts… talking to them, asking opinions…"

The room fell silent. Ken was giving her all the space she needed.

Late afternoon sunshine glinted on the window frame.

Mixed emotions stirred.

Dread.

And relief.

"Jamie…"

She told him everything. Not just of the loss, but of the ongoing connection to what might have been.

Another silence ensued before Ken spoke softly.

"That's two of us with a hole in our lives then."

"Yes."

"Have you told Gus?"

"No. I've never told anyone until now."

"Then you're right not to tell him. Not until you're absolutely sure the relationship is going somewhere."

She nodded.

"I ought to be going," she said.

"Right… could you get me some bits from home? Some extra-soft tissues, my soft mints, and my wallet from the top left drawer in the front room."

"No problem at all, Ken."

As a nurse came in to check on the patient, Olivia squeezed her old friend's hand.

34

In Other Times

Olivia was sitting quietly on the patio with the sun setting on the far side of the fields beyond the vineyard. Luke would stay with Gus overnight, mindful of the shock she'd had – and maybe feeling a little out of his depth in being able to offer comfort. Gus had suggested he and Luke stay at her place, but she assured him she was glad of the quiet.

Taking a sip of wine, she thought of Ken and wondered about Maybrook in the old days. What had it been like in the early 60s? Or earlier, when Ken came down from London during the War?

On a whim, she fetched her laptop and looked up old maps of the area. A beautifully detailed one dating from 1925 showed that not much had changed in Maybrook during the past century.

She tried earlier – Roman times.

That didn't help much. The place was unrecognizable.

So, what about somewhere in between, when her family were involved in the founding of the village itself?

She found something interesting on an antiquarian dealer's website – a map dating from circa 1640 that had recently been obtained from a private collection in London. The Old Hall, dating back to 1604, was there – with a few smaller buildings around it. Across the road, there was an inn, which appeared to be an earlier version of the Royal Standard. There were also houses down an unnamed lane that had to be Southway. However, there was no sign of Colshot Lane. The entire area was farmland. There were lines here and there – lanes, probably – but it wasn't possible to zoom in.

She checked the web page details. It seemed the retailer wanted money. Seven whole pounds for a high-resolution download.

No way.

She continued to stare and squint. It made no difference. The details on the map wouldn't play ball.

"Okay, you win."

She went through the motions with a credit card and got the download. A moment later, on her laptop screen, she found where the yet-to-exist Colshot Lane would come into being and zoomed in a little closer.

"Right…"

She ran her finger along from the main highway, past 'farm' – which pre-dated her 1862-built house by two centuries. It was difficult to match things to modern Maybrook, but…

Her finger stopped where she might have expected to see a north-south line that would become Potter's Lane. It wasn't there.

But while neither Potter's Lane nor Colshot Lane yet existed…

"That's odd…"

A little farther on, her finger stopped at an unnamed

north-south line, which later centuries would come to know as Hopton Way. And now, a whole new story opened up.

35

Sunday

Olivia's Sunday morning phone call to the hospital elicited a response that Ken would be kept in under observation for the time being, but that she could visit. Despite that, she wanted to know how he looked, his mood, their prognosis – but none of these details were forthcoming.

She checked in with Sue and Cam who were looking after Beano, and then headed over to Ken's place to pick up a few bits. Standing in his front room, she felt a sense of calm – unlike the panic of yesterday when she had felt ill with worry. She could feel his presence and all but hear his voice. The house was silent though. Incredibly silent.

She turned to the photos on his mantelpiece. One was of Ken's parents on their wedding day not far short of a century ago. Their poverty wasn't fully concealed – their faces were thin and drawn in, their clothes not quite fitting.

The photo of Ken in his army uniform was impressive. She could sense the post-War years, with young recruits required to do two years National Service and go to all parts of the world.

She wondered about teenage love. He'd gone into the army at eighteen. He and Gloria… well, Ken had made the point that they had definitely been attracted to one other. Except she ended up marrying Charlie. The attraction didn't fade though, because in 1962… well, Ken said it wasn't loose morals. He and Gloria simply looked at each other and… they couldn't help it.

She smiled and went to get the few bits he'd asked for. She added a few things to the list of extra soft tissues and soft mints. A dressing gown for one.

Almost done, she went to get his wallet from the old walnut cabinet in the front room.

Sliding open the top left drawer, she was faced with a large manilla envelope. It was marked 'Alice'.

She hesitated and pondered her options. Then she peeked inside.

There were photos, school reports, and a number of music certificates, one of which she studied a little closer.

She recognized the name of the certifier.

*

At the hospital, Olivia found Ken sitting up in bed reading a newspaper. He put it down as soon as he saw her.

"You didn't have to visit again," he said.

"I'm not visiting, I'm bringing you some of your things. How are you feeling?"

"Mustn't grumble," he said. He looked his ninety years, but the spirit was still there. "How's Luke?"

Don't change the subject, Ken…

"He's okay."

She handed him his soft tissues and soft mints. His dressing gown, she placed on the end of the bed.

"Thanks," he said. He opened the pack of mints and took one. "Luke told me about a local office hub idea. Now, that's not something I understand a great deal, but I do know it's something that would work in Maybrook."

He offered Olivia a mint, but she declined.

"I'm not sure he's thought it through, Ken."

"He's in contact with a woman whose husband works for a City firm. They're looking to scale back on office space. They have a dozen or so people who live within twenty minutes' drive of Maybrook. Some of them don't wish to work from home for a variety of reasons. The hub would be a small office for four or five people. More if a suitable site had a little development potential."

"Okay, so he *has* thought it through."

"Why don't you find the perfect location for Luke's hub idea."

"The perfect location?"

"Yes, the perfect location."

"Yes, okay, but… could we get back to you asking me to get your things."

"Any particular reason?"

"I saw Alice's envelope. You obviously wanted me to."

"I rescued it from Gloria's house after she died. Did you have a look through everything?"

"No, I took a peek but there's personal stuff in there. I wanted to check with you first. I wanted you to give me permission first-hand."

"Of course you can look. That was the point."

"Do you think Gloria would mind?"

Ken thought about that for a moment.

"My gut feeling is… she wouldn't have wanted Alice to be forgotten. We occasionally went over to the cemetery. You know, to think of her and keep her memory alive."

"You *and* Gloria?"

"Now it's just me – obviously."

So now we know who left the flowers…

Olivia went to the window. There wasn't much to see apart from a wood pigeon patrolling a small patch of grass.

"You said you didn't think she loved you. But you loved her though."

"How could anyone not love Gloria? Or at least feel for her. If they knew her… I mean *really* knew her."

The pigeon flew off. Olivia tracked it over the building opposite until it vanished into the blue.

"People say she was difficult to get on with."

"People…" huffed Ken. "Gloria was a country girl at heart. Whereas most see the summer as June, July, August… she saw it as strawberries, cherries, early plums… and the year would carry on as pears, apples, hops, grapes, potatoes…"

Olivia turned away from the window to face him.

"That's lovely, Ken. I never got that impression."

"It was her family who insisted she be a proper lady with clean fingernails and an interest in charity committees and middle-class dinner parties. Somewhere in between all that, I think she got lost."

Olivia tried to imagine it.

"And what about you? Did you always live in Colshot Lane?"

"No, I lived down the bottom of Southway for a while, but the property was condemned because of damp and rot. I moved to Colshot Lane in the late 50s."

"Before Gloria and Charlie moved in just across the lane?"

"Gloria's parents lived at Whitman Farm then. I rented a place nearby simply because it was available. And I ended up buying it."

"How was Charlie? I mean what with you and

Gloria…"

"We got along just fine. Gloria and me was behind us, so to speak. Alice was growing up elsewhere and life went on."

"It must have been awkward."

"Yes, but I wasn't going to move house. I was living in Colshot Lane before Charlie. Besides, my respect for Gloria made sure there was no unpleasantness."

"Your take on the simple life is certainly complicated."

"Perhaps."

"What about Raymond?"

"He worked for Gloria. We all knew him from way back, of course, but he didn't play much of a role."

Not for the first time, Olivia's mind wandered back to the letter behind Gloria's photo.

"I'm pleased you've taken an interest in Alice," said Ken.

"Pleased?"

"I wanted it kept private, but… well… there was a moment when I decided to tell you everything, but then I changed my mind to help you."

"I don't understand."

"I could see you were feeling something – the beginnings of a bond, if you like. I decided if I left you to find out things for yourself, Alice would mean more to you. If you're not sure what I mean, ask your friend Katy how she feels about her Victorian ancestors."

"Katy?"

"Yes, ask her."

*

Back at home, among the vines, Olivia acknowledged that Gloria would have left everything to her daughter. All this would have belonged to Alice, and that felt right.

But fate had taken a hand and Olivia had been given this chance. And to her, down from London, the opportunity to make a new life was now more precious than ever.

She moved farther into the vineyard.

All this…

Had fate taken a different course, there would have been no phone call from Jo the solicitor and no escaping Prior Grove. In a single moment back in the late 1980s, Alice handed Olivia, Sue, and Milo something that would echo down the years until it could form into a new beginning.

Gus phoned and she updated him on Ken's health. She also mentioned Luke's office hub idea.

"I'm not sure about that, Liv. And as for Luke, he's gone back to Beth."

Olivia sagged.

"Right…"

She decided to push the hub idea, but not over the phone. She'd see Gus in person. Beforehand though, there was someone else she needed to see first.

Following a quick shower and a change of clothes, Olivia arrived at Katy's home. She updated her on Ken and promised to relay Katy and Steve's best wishes.

"There was something else," Olivia said.

She couldn't tell Katy about her search for Alice and how she believed Ken to be involved. She needed another way.

"Go on," said Katy.

"Silly really, but we got talking about genealogy. I said I wasn't sure if to invest the time finding out about my lot. I've heard a few stories, but Ken said if I wanted to get to know them, to ask you how you feel about your Victorian ancestors."

"I think I know what he means," said Katy. "Years ago, my gran told me about my family in the 1930s. It was lovely to hear, but it felt distant and second-hand. I mentioned it to Ken. He said the past is gone, but if we do our own research, bonds can form between us and those no longer here."

"Okay…"

"So, I spent a lot of time looking into my ancestors from the late Victorian period. One girl, Sarah… I followed her out of Mile End in London, into hospital for whooping cough, through school, through her job as a worker in a match factory where girls were dying of phosphorous poisoning… and I wanted to reach back in time and tell her that everything would be alright. She died aged thirty-two. She was my great, great grandmother's big sister, but she's so much more than that to me."

Olivia smiled. She understood.

Katy's expression was warm and sincere.

"You might think it's daft," she said, "but she's in my heart."

"Katy, I absolutely do not think it's daft."

Olivia cared about Alice, that was for certain. Was Alice in her heart? Yes, she was.

Ken, you old rascal.

36

It's All New To Me

"An office hub in my apartment?"

The concept, now fully explained, still baffled Gus.

At the lounge window, Olivia peered out over the road below. All was Sunday quiet. For a moment, she wondered what Luke was up to. Then she turned to face the room and tried to see it as a hub. There would need to be a proper makeover… but yes. It certainly beat her old firm Prior Grove for charm. People working here would become friends. They would stroll to the pub for lunch or maybe bring a sandwich and walk through the nearby fields to work off the calories.

Gus would find a new home at Whitman Farm. She didn't care much for his furniture, but it was fine. She wouldn't be laying down any rules on that score. There was plenty of room.

She plonked herself down on the car seat sofa. Bella rose from her cushion and came to sit by her, leaning against her leg.

"A hub?" he mulled. "Won't it be a bit crowded?"

"Not if you remove the wall between the lounge and the bedroom."

"Where would I sleep?"

"In the garage or maybe in a field. Or you could move in with me."

"I see."

"It's what Luke – at least I think I'm right… it's possibly what he would like now he's got to see everyone's issues from all sides."

Gus raised an eyebrow. "Are you saying Luke has been working on a way to fix my business problems?"

"While we've been working out a way to fix his life, he's come up with the best idea for you. The rent would keep you from going further into debt."

"It all seems a bit sudden."

"Yes, so…?"

"I hate Luke knowing about my problems."

"He has eyes and ears. Once he started staying over, he was always going to see how things are."

Gus sighed.

"Look," said Olivia, "how about we go for a walk."

"You've only just got here. No, actually, you go. I need to do some thinking."

"Shall I stay then? We could have lunch here."

"No, it's okay. I'm not sure what I need to think about yet."

"We can't live like this," said Olivia.

"No."

They fell into a prolonged silence.

"How about I show you a map?" Olivia eventually said.

"Hmm," said Gus with a twinkle in his eye. "I don't usually need a map."

"Just concentrate for two minutes."

A moment later, Gus was transfixed by the old map on her phone's screen.

"So, Colshot Lane would come into being here," she said, running her finger along from a thick line that was now the main road and past 'farm'. "Then this is where Potter's Lane is today. If we follow it north to the bridge…"

"There's nothing there," said Gus. "No bridge, no lane…"

"Just this." She pointed to a small square marked 'pottery'. "So, if we move across to where today's Hopton Way exists… and if we go north…"

"Hopton Way wasn't a dead end."

"Not a bridge," said Olivia, "but a ford."

"The stories I've heard go back to Victorian times. As I understood it, the stone bridge replaced an earlier wooden one."

"It obviously did," said Olivia. "But that clearly wasn't the original crossing point. This map is hundreds of years before all that. If we go up to where Forest Edge is today… and to Ralston… you can see it's a straight road all the way from Hopton Way."

She pointed to just south of where the Forest Edge development was now rising.

"Today's road curves to meet the bridge that takes us into Potter's Lane."

"That's interesting," said Gus. "But what does it mean?"

"I haven't got to the best bit yet," said Olivia.

She took them back along Hopton Way.

"Opposite here is where Alan Curtis-Fisher lives. In 1640, there was no estate. But there was an unmarked lane."

Her finger ran slowly along the lane.

"This is all new to me," said Gus. "Can you make the map any bigger?"

"No, sorry. You'll have to squint."

He followed Olivia's finger as it continued south.

"That's the boundary of Tony's land," she said.

Her finger continued.

"And that would be the boundary with Whitman Farm."

Olivia's finger continued before finally coming to a halt.

"Oh," said Gus. "The Royal Standard."

"Fascinating or what?"

"So, when that lane disappeared… it must have been a land grab," said Gus. "Cheeky old Moorcroft's – or at least their ancestors."

"Exactly," said Olivia. "Perhaps the time has come for them to hand it back to the public."

"Um… isn't Curtis-Fisher's estate in the way?"

"Trust you to spot the flaw. The thing is we can't have the cycle way going on Tony's land. His house is right by the boundary. He'd have people walking and cycling right past the front door. And if we come back the other side of his house, we'd cut him off from his field."

Gus nodded. "If you go round the far side of Curtis-Fisher's land, you'll be going miles out of your way. And you'd hit Moorcroft's sheds and stuff. There'd be tractors and cyclists…"

"It needs to go inside Curtis Fisher's boundary with Tony's patch. Then it's a dead-straight line from Hopton Way to the Royal Standard."

"It works for me," said Gus. "All you have to do is get Alan to say, hey, what a great idea!"

Olivia put her phone down and picked up the photo album. This would have a good spot on the bookshelf in the lounge at Whitman Farm, she hoped.

She opened it.

She once told Gus he was so lucky to have captured such wonderful memories of Luke growing up.

She thought of Jamie.

To have a photo album…

She imagined it:

Jamie, 4, with a tennis racket that was too big; Jamie, 6, playing with a Lego set; Jamie, 11, with a certificate for Excellence in Literature…

Would she have made a good parent? There was no way to know, of course. Luke was a young man at the start of his life. Was helping him a pain? Or was it a privilege?

"I really love these photos," she said. "Especially this one."

Gus took a closer look.

"Why that one?"

37

The Plan

Forty minutes later, just outside Maidstone, Olivia pulled off the main road into a small estate of bungalows where every front garden was in bloom.

She stopped outside one and went up to the front door. It opened just as her finger reached for the bell.

"Hi," said Beth. "Come in. Gus was a bit vague…"

"That's my fault. He wasn't quite up to speed, but I didn't want to turn up unannounced."

Olivia joined her in the lounge, where Luke was waiting.

"Tea? Or Coffee?" Beth asked.

"Tea, thanks," said Olivia, taking a seat – although hardly sitting back into the comfy armchair. More perched bird-like on its edge, ready for flight.

"Luke?" said Beth.

"I'm fine, thanks."

Beth smiled and then disappeared to make the tea.

"I thought some more about the future," said Luke. "I worked it out."

"You worked out the future?"

"It's like organizing a brilliant party for the week after next. You hire a hall, put together a guest list, book a DJ, and sort out the food and drinks. You anticipate, worry, fret and generally get anxious. Then you go along telling yourself it's going to be amazing…"

"And?"

"When you get to the hall, there's a notice pinned to the door telling you that the party has moved to another hall and that most of the guests will be different. The DJ is now a band that plays music you don't like, and the food and drink is different. Oh, and you're not dressed for whatever kind of party it's turned into."

Olivia gathered her wits.

"You know, sometimes, that party you arranged – sometimes that would be the dullest, most boring, predictable party ever. And sometimes, the new party… that's where you might meet interesting people... and maybe because you're not listening to the music all night, you might get to meet someone important. The upshot, Luke, is that we have very little control over our lives, okay? We do our best to keep our options open, but we do not paralyze ourselves by fretting over every single detail in advance. And sometimes we just have to get out there, and say eff it, let's do this!"

Luke eyed her with suspicion. And then, gradually, with a smile.

"I was hoping you might say something like that."

"All part of the service."

"I'm sorry I rushed off. It was just with Ken in hospital… I felt a bit scared and awkward."

"Me too."

And I'm not fifteen…

She puffed out her cheeks.

"Look, Ken's going to be okay. How about we concentrate on something else."

Luke brightened. "Okay, so what's the plan?"

"I'll explain it on the way."

"The way to where?"

"You'll see."

Olivia apologised profusely to Beth, explaining that something urgent had come up. Luke confirmed that he needed to go with Olivia, and both left Beth looking confused but waving all the same.

As they drove off, Luke was eager for knowledge.

"So – the plan?"

"You go first. This hub idea? We seem to be at a point where Gus's apartment is the logical place for it. And we seem to have at least one person interested. That would mean your dad having nowhere to live unless he moves in with me."

Luke said nothing.

"And there's me thinking *I'm* the dark arts master," she concluded.

"Now it's your turn," said Luke. "The plan?"

"You're right. We have work to do!"

"So…?"

"You might have given us a cost-effective way forward. Local authorities and developers like the term 'cost-effective'. It guarantees a project gets a fair hearing."

"Okay…"

"I mean we're two outsiders hoping our contribution is valid when the idea is the thing."

"Keep going."

"It should always be about the idea – the *best* idea regardless of who came up with it. Anything else will hold the village back."

"Or even the world?"

Olivia took a moment and then glanced across at Luke. "Are you up for this?"

"You still haven't told me the plan."

*

Olivia pulled up outside a neat semi-detached house on the northern edge of Folkestone. Aaron Price, structural engineer opened the door to them.

"Sorry to bother you on a Sunday afternoon," said Olivia.

"I was a little surprised by your text…"

"Yes, your number was on some papers relating to the new bridge."

"Well… come in."

He showed them into the hallway where they said a quick hello to his wife at the kitchen door. Aaron then directed them into the lounge.

"Take a seat."

"Thanks," said Olivia.

"Tea? Coffee?"

"No, we're fine," said Olivia. "We won't stop long. As an engineer, we'd value your opinion on something."

"I'm usually reached for potential commissions via the company's offices."

"Yes, but as you were kind enough to give us your home address…"

"You said it was important."

Olivia showed him a photo on her phone screen. It was from ten years back – Luke playing with Lego bricks.

"Could we do this with the old stone bridge?"

"Play with it?"

"Yes, play with it. Dismantle it. Put it back together again."

"Just a little way downstream," Luke added.

"Have you spoken to anyone about it? The District Council, perhaps?"

"Not yet. We thought we'd start with the parish council. If they support it, we'll have the best possible way to influence the big hitters."

"Yes, I suppose so. They're more likely to commit to something if they know it'll be popular."

"So, moving the bridge. Luke and I are ready to volunteer. We could number each stone with paint to make it easier to reassemble. If that helps?"

Aaron smiled in a slightly surprised way.

"It's a nice idea but not necessary. It would be a lot easier to simply build a new bridge."

"We'd like to preserve the heritage aspect."

"You will – but it has to be rebuilt as new. Remember, the current bridge dates back a couple of centuries, but the stones probably date back a hundred million years."

"Right, so we don't paint numbers on each one..."

"There's really no need. We would group the salvaged stones in terms of size and shape. The finished bridge would look incredibly similar to the current one."

"How do you build a stone bridge?" Olivia asked.

"It's quite straightforward. You create a concrete platform either side the stream. Then... if you imagine the space beneath the arch where the water runs – you build a solid timber and plywood formwork to fill that space. Hang on..."

He disappeared into the kitchen.

Olivia and Luke exchanged a look.

A moment later, Aaron returned with a bottle of beer.

Olivia and Luke exchanged another look.

Aaron placed the bottle on its side on the coffee table.

"That's our formwork. Now we lay our stones on top

of it. Could one of you lay all the stones over the formwork, locked together tight like a jigsaw puzzle."

Before Olivia and Luke could exchange a third glance, Aaron continued.

"A hand will do."

Luke placed his hand over the bottle… which Aaron then slid out, leaving Luke's hand, or the stones, forming a perfect arch.

"Obviously, that's a bit simplistic," said Aaron, "but you get the idea."

Olivia wasn't too sure. "Won't it collapse?"

"If the stones are packed tight, at the right angle, with a keystone at the high point of the arch, then no. All the pressure will be the two sides of the bridge pushing against each other. The Romans were doing this two thousand years ago."

"I like it," said Luke.

"It's certainly amazing," said Olivia.

"There's another consideration though," said Aaron. "How do you propose to get the parish council behind the idea?"

"Using dark arts," said Luke.

Olivia smiled. "He means we'll think of something."

*

Just after seven, Olivia and Luke were at Sue and Cam's. A bottle of rhubarb wine was already open.

"Sue, we once said we needed a safe cycle and pedestrian route from Forest Edge."

"That hasn't changed," said Sue.

"I think you should stand."

Hesitantly, Sue raised herself from the sofa.

"No," said Olivia. "I mean you should stand in the

election."

"Oh… but wouldn't we split the vote for our ideas?"

"I'm not standing."

"Why not?" said Sue, sitting once more.

"We need someone with genuine passion. My interests are Whitman Farm and wine. Yours are much more community based."

Olivia's thoughts momentarily filled with hanging baskets, cakes and pies.

"Are you sure?" said Sue.

"Yes, I'm sure."

Sue took a moment to collect her thoughts.

"Right, well… thank you, Olivia. With your support, I'd like to give it a go."

"Fantastic."

Cam was beaming.

"I think it's a wonderful idea."

"Do you really think I can win?" Sue asked.

It was a good question.

"We'll need to pull Son of Colin's rug," said Olivia. "We'll need the council to shift their support in your direction."

"How?"

"Cam, what dirt have you got on council members?"

Cam looked surprised.

"None."

"Come on."

"No, honestly."

"Have more wine."

"Well… one of them is cheating on his wife…"

"Go on…"

"And one is under a tax investigation."

"Don't stop…"

"You can't do this."

Olivia relented.

"You're right, I can't. We'll have to think of something else."

*

An hour later, Olivia and Luke were back at Whitman Farm making a fuss of Bella.

"Would it be okay to take her for a walk?" Luke asked.

"Oh… great. Brilliant. Yes. Over the bridge is best but keep her on the leash until you're in Potter's Lane."

She watched them go and couldn't help but smile.

Progress.

A moment later, she faced Gloria's photo on the lounge wall.

"Whitman Farm is still working its magic," she told the former owner.

She took an envelope from the bookcase. The photos, school reports, music certificates… Alice was more alive than ever.

Olivia returned to Gloria's photo.

"I still don't really know you, Gloria, but you'll be having company soon. No, this isn't about Gus and Luke – someone very close to you is about to get a lot closer. You'll see."

Her phone rang.

She didn't recognise the number.

"Hello?"

"Is that you, Olivia? It's Ken."

"Ken? How are you?"

"They're satisfied the fall was down to low blood pressure. They've given me a lot of advice and some pills. Could you come and pick me up? They said I can come home."

Olivia whooped. It took a moment to explain to Ken that she hadn't had a seizure and that she'd be there before he knew it.

38

Busy, Busy!

It was the first Monday of the school summer holidays. Six long weeks that would no doubt flash by. So, of all the things that Luke might do, Olivia was pleased when he offered to accompany her on a visit to Ken across the lane.

Ken was delighted to see them both, just as Beano was pleased to see Bella. To Olivia, seeing him seated in his usual chair in his own front room – he was looking so much better.

"So how are you and Dad getting on?" he asked Luke.

"We're doing okay, thanks."

"That's good to hear. Being a dad is a funny old role, but parents are always proud of their children."

Luke nodded. "Um… how about I make us some coffee?"

Ken and Olivia exchanged a smile as he headed for the kitchen.

"He's a good lad," said Ken.

"Yes, he is. Did you know he plays the flute?"

"No…?"

"His music tutor was Fliss Fairfax."

"Oh?"

"You might remember her. She taught Alice."

"Did she?"

"According to those certificates, Alice was a White Horse Music Association Scholarship student."

"Interesting."

"I looked them up, Ken. Not a trace of them anywhere. One music teacher I spoke to said he'd never heard of them. I suppose some charitable benefactors got together to pay for music lessons for budding talents."

Ken shrugged. "Well, maybe one."

"An anonymous benefactor. No fanfares?"

"I knew someone who could print some headed paper for me. There was no need to see Alice. It was all arranged through a tutor without anyone meeting me personally. Did you know the white horse is our county's symbol?"

"Yes, but… why didn't Gloria volunteer to teach her?"

"This was way back when she was six. By the time she played with Gloria and the others, Alice was a star. At least, she could have been had she wanted to. But she was a country girl at heart. She loved sharing music with friends and family. That was it."

"A country girl at heart? Where have I heard that before?"

"It's like I said. I did what I could from the side. She was free to be whoever she wanted to be."

Olivia nodded.

"I'd like to put a framed photo of Alice on the wall next to Gloria. What do you think?"

"I think it's the right thing to do. It never occurred to me that someone might think fondly of Alice from time to time once I've gone. I'm glad you've taken an interest."

"Poked my nose in, you mean?"

Ken eyes glistened. "You know a little about Gloria. Not much, but more than most. And now you know something about Alice. As curator of Whitman Farm's history, you've made a very promising start."

Olivia squeezed his hand.

"Thanks Ken."

A few minutes later, Luke returned with the coffee.

"Time to reveal the map," said Olivia, pulling a roll of paper from her bag.

"Map?" said Ken.

"Right," said Luke. "We printed a copy."

They unfurled the paper version of the old map and began pointing out key features to Ken. Then they unrolled a paper copy of modern Maybrook and did likewise.

"The road from Forest Edge will be widened and go over the new bridge as planned," said Olivia.

"The district council's paying for that," said Luke.

"Then Potter's Lane will be widened."

"The district council's paying for that too."

"Then traffic will turn into the widened section of Colshot Lane, continue onto the new section, and join with the main road."

"So, now the good bit," said Luke. "Starting again, back at Forest Edge, we'll have a cycle and pedestrian lane run parallel to the existing road for fifty yards."

"I see," said Ken.

"Then," continued Luke, "where the road curves to line up with the new bridge, a cycle way will run in a straight line to the new crossing point."

"Except it's not new," said Olivia. "It was the original crossing point."

"Is that where a reconstituted stone bridge goes?" Ken asked.

"Yes."

"The developer can pay for that. They're duty bound to add an amenity."

"Then," said Luke, "we'll have the pedestrian and cycle way continue along Hopton Way to Colshot Lane, where we'll install a pedestrian crossing."

"The district council can pay for that," said Ken.

Olivia took over. "The pedestrian and cycle way follows the ancient way – cutting through Alan Curtis-Fisher's side bit, across the back of Cam's brother's land and across the back of Whitman Farm."

"With a new nature reserve right across Whitman Farm's rear boundary," Luke added.

"And a new fence with a gate in it," said Olivia. "We'll have our own short cut to the village."

Ken was studying the details.

"So, continuing past your place?"

"The path goes along the edge of some small private parcels of land – and then it pops out by the Royal Standard."

"That's a triumph," said Ken. "Assuming Moorcroft's and Alan Curtis-Fisher agree."

"If they do, there'll be a new crossing on the High Street," said Olivia. "Then it's a hop, skip, and a jump to the school."

"Where we'll have a bicycle parking area for schoolchildren and shoppers," Luke added.

Ken nodded his approval.

"You've done well."

"Thanks," said Olivia.

"So now you post copies of the route through every letterbox."

"Yes," said Olivia.

"No," said Luke. "You're forgetting something – we

understand the dark arts. We get parish council members to knock on each door and hand one over in person."

Olivia was as surprised as Ken.

"How?" she asked.

*

Half an hour later, Olivia, Luke, Bella and Beano were heading down Colshot Lane – Ken having been left behind for a well-earned rest. They passed the corner of Potter's Lane and continued on to the corner of Hopton Way, where Olivia studied the Curtis-Fisher residence anew.

They just needed a certain individual to see it their way.

They headed along Hopton Way, enjoying the quiet all the way to the water. The only sound was a quiet discussion about the plan for the bridge.

"It's going to be great," said Luke.

"There's still a bit of politics to do first," said Olivia. "We need support."

Reaching the stream, they made their way along the bank back to the old stone bridge. There they climbed the bank and strode onto the structure for what they supposed might be the last time.

Olivia was waving two small sticks.

Luke's eyes widened in alarm. "You must be joking."

"You're a mature fifteen-year-old. You can play pooh sticks without fear."

"Won't Bella jump in after them?"

"Not if we throw this." It was an even bigger stick that Olivia threw into the open land north of the bridge. Bella raced off after it. Beano decided to sit by their feet instead.

Luke shook his head. "If anyone sees me…"

"The world would end?"

"You do realise you won't win?"

"Prepare to suffer!"

They played out a keenly contested series, interrupted only by taking turns to give Bella something to chase. The main event ended in a two-two stalemate.

"One more for the winner?" Luke suggested.

"Let's shake hands on a tied game."

They did so.

"Two titans of the sport," said Luke.

"Definitely. There should be TV highlights."

"Pay per view?"

"Absolutely."

Olivia marvelled that their relationship wasn't yet two months old. She hadn't exactly taken to him at first, but a little patience had transformed everything.

Was there any sign of a hug from Luke?

They settled for a high five.

39

Sue & Cam's Wedding

The very end of July blessed Maybrook with clear blue skies and warm sunshine.

At the church on Saturday just before two, Sue, in shimmering sky blue, and Cam, in a new dark blue suit, soaked up the goodwill of sixty well-wishers. The rehearsal two days earlier had been straightforward. Olivia, as maid of honour, performed her main task once they got home – when she cracked open a bottle of Sauvignon Blanc for her and Sue to enjoy. Today, there wasn't much to do but enjoy the occasion.

Milo and his girlfriend Ruth were there. It was so good to see them. When Olivia went over to say hello, Milo was telling Ruth that a big part of village life was that nothing much happened. Olivia happily concurred, although her thoughts flicked through Gus, Luke, Ken, Alice, Bella, standing for the parish council, campaigning to save a bridge, attending wine classes and performing in a video.

While Ruth got sucked into a conversation with Annie,

Olivia introduced Milo to Luke, who was quickly curious about Milo's work in Canterbury.

Inside the church, Olivia took in the background organ music, the gorgeous stained-glass window, the vivid floral display by the altar, and the smell of the polished oak pews.

Along with the beaming vicar and best man Tony, she welcomed the congregation.

Ted and Tom wheeled Ken in, although he insisted on walking the final few steps to his seat – one strictly allotted to him by Olivia, on the basis that it was next to a certain music teacher who once spent ten years on an inter-parish committee with Cam.

Olivia leaned over to do the introductions.

"Ken, this is Fliss Fairfax. Fliss, this is the White Horse Music Association."

Fliss laughed. "We're actually old friends."

"Old and very good friends," said Ken with a twinkle in his eye.

Fliss grinned. "We once went to a music festival where the accommodation was double booked. We ended up sharing a tent for three days!"

Ken winked at Olivia.

Olivia tactfully moved off to help someone, anyone who needed it.

Katy caught her eye.

"I spoke to Moorcroft's this morning. They've agreed to the plan."

"Oh, that's brilliant," said Olivia. "We're getting closer."

The wedding service was short but perfect – just as Sue and Cam had planned. Everyone sang Amazing Grace and enjoyed Killy's warm reading of poems by Rossetti and Shelley.

The 'I do' moment was met with smiles and sighs of

contentment, perhaps mainly for Cam who most knew had struggled with being alone before Sue came along.

Outside, everyone posed for photos – both official and an extra few hundred on a myriad of phones. That said, Sue made sure the official photographer got a good one of her, Olivia and Milo. The three newcomers. Down from London. And now Kent folk, through and through.

"I was thinking the hub's a good idea," Gus acknowledged to Olivia when they got a moment together. He'd clearly been mulling it over. "I mean the garage can't go on forever. Ten years from now, there won't be enough old cars around – just battery-operated computers on wheels that drive themselves."

"Maybe it's time to talk to the bank," said Olivia. "A business loan would help you convert the whole place."

Gus nodded and brushed her cheek softly with his hand.

"I… um… I should say this more often, but I do love you from top to toe and I'm sorry it's been a tough couple of months."

She squeezed his hand. "I love you too, and I can assure you everything is fine."

Twenty minutes later, everyone was making the short walk to the Old Hall.

"Lovely weather," Katy's dad, Steve said to Olivia.

"It really does help," she acknowledged.

"Cam's first wedding… well, there was a downpour. Nearly washed half the congregation down the High Street."

Olivia smiled and felt both happy and sad for Cam. But mainly happy – today was aimed squarely at the future. Nobody was going to forget the past, but sometimes it had to be held in its place.

The caterers had decked out the Old Hall beautifully,

with confetti-strewn tables laden with puff pastry cheese bakes, roasted pepper tarts, spicy chicken wings, barbecue spare-ribs and various salads, rice dishes and French sticks – and, of course, a truckload of pastries and desserts.

Arrivals were handed a glass of chilled fizz – not any old supermarket wine, but Whitman Farm's very own sparkling. The popping of corks was music to Olivia's ears. And, more importantly, the taste on the tongue was light and refreshing, just as fizz should be. When she and Sue clinked glasses, they paused a moment to let the magnitude of the achievement sink in. It raced through Olivia's mind: from pruning in winter to bud-rubbing in spring. From flowering to veraison. And harvesting with a small army of volunteers.

"Cheers, Sue. Let's always be grateful for good fortune."

"Yes, well, I believe you have work to do."

"You're right, I do – now, where's my co-conspirator?"

Olivia found Luke by the side of the small stage.

"Time to say hi to Councillor Miller," she said. "Cam says he loves talking about his garden."

Luke nodded and they moved in. Their target was engaged, as planned, in idle chatter with Katy. She acknowledged them and made the introductions.

"Such lovely weather," said Olivia. "It's almost a shame to be inside. I'm envious of anyone working in their garden right now…"

"Are you a gardener?" he asked.

"Outside of vineyard duties, I'm looking to improve the bit of garden I have. I'm not sure what grows best in the local soil though. Is that something you would know about?"

Olivia, Luke and Katy smiled and nodded a lot over the following ten minutes as Councillor Miller took them on a horticultural journey of the ideal Kentish Garden while Olivia kept his glass topped up.

"Amazing stuff," said Olivia. "We're looking to create some garden spaces on a cycle and pedestrian way from Forest Edge to the Royal Standard. Obviously, there are hurdles, but we're hopeful. Is that something you would support – a cycle and pedestrian route with shrubs and so on to help define the path's borders?"

"Well, it sounds… yes… if it's possible, absolutely."

Olivia and Luke tactfully but swiftly moved on to their next target, where Katy's dad, Steve had already cornered Councillor Austin. According to Cam, he was an absolute nut for Crystal Palace Football Club.

No sooner had Steve introduced them, Luke moved into action.

"I can't wait for the new football season to start. I'm a Crystal Palace fan, for my sins…"

The following ten minutes flashed by in a haze of past glories and future hopes before Olivia came in with the potential for the cycle and walking route to provide a simple but brilliant way for children and adults to stay healthy.

The campaign continued in a similar vein for an hour or so before Olivia and Luke agreed they had done everything possible to get things moving.

"Just one more nut to crack," said Olivia.

"The big one," said Luke.

"The final push for victory."

"Do or die."

Olivia took a fortifying breath. No matter which way she looked at it, a viable pathway would require a two-hundred-foot strip of Alan Curtis-Fisher's land along its border with Tony's farm.

She focused. This was it.

"Let's go."

She moved directly into Alan's sphere. He was talking with Robin the historian about the snow in Sydney, Australia. She did her best to get in on the conversation, but he seemed determined to be exclusively fascinated by Robin's observations.

"Robin!" cried Katy, intercepting to divert the historian's attention. "What are your views on senior citizens trips to Roman sites? I'm thinking of organizing one to Lullingstone Villa…"

With Robin effectively neutralized for hours, possibly even days, Olivia made her move.

"A new pathway," she said. "From Forest Edge to the Royal Standard…"

"I'm not quite with you," said Alan, seemingly a little puzzled.

Olivia went into full-on public relations mode, flagging up all the benefits of the brand new and yet historically ancient route into the village. Alan became increasingly interested… until his own contribution came up. Any enthusiasm dissipated at that point.

"It would be wonderful for the village," Olivia insisted.

"I'm sure we can do better," he said.

"I don't think you can," said Olivia. "This really is the best plan."

"There'll be other options once I've had a chance to think."

Alan withdrew and Olivia felt the tide turning away from them. Son of Colin would win the election. A majority of members would speak on his behalf. Sue had no chance. Unless…

Unless?

There was no 'unless.'

She shrugged at Luke, who seemed… frustrated?

Angry? No, his look was one of determination.

"Back me up, Olivia."

"What?"

"And buckle up. It could get bumpy."

Luke produced the old map from his pocket.

"Mr Curtis-Fisher…?"

Olivia followed Luke as he intercepted the target and persuaded him to step outside, away from prying eyes and ears.

"What's this about?" Alan demanded.

"It's about Curtis-Fisher Way," Luke explained.

"About what?"

"It's the name Olivia came up with for the cycle way."

Alan had the look of a man caught off-guard as he turned to Olivia.

"You never said…?"

"No," said Olivia, rapidly reordering her thoughts. "No… but there's a reason for that." *Which I'll invent in a couple of seconds.* "Basically, Luke and I… we felt… it might be best… if we…"

"Kept it secret," said Luke.

"Yes, kept it secret… for now," said Olivia. "It'll be called Curtis-Fisher Way, but we can't announce it yet. We'll get Sue to propose it. You can look completely shocked and surprised and then delighted. It'll go through on the nod."

"Sue?"

"We can't really ask anyone else."

"Sue… yes, I suppose she's an asset to the community. Possibly, the sort of dedicated person we need."

"You could set up a sub-committee," said Olivia. "You wouldn't personally be part of it, but Sue would. She could make the suggestion from there."

"Curtis-Fisher Way," said Alan Curtis-Fisher, relishing

each and every syllable.

"But not a word to anyone," said Olivia. "Not even to Sue."

A few moments later, back in the hall, Olivia wondered.

"Should we mention any of this to Sue?"

Luke shrugged. "Mention any of what?"

Gus came over to join them.

"It's shaping up to be quite a wedding," he said.

"It certainly is," said Olivia.

Luke smiled at her. "You and Dad next?"

Olivia felt fit to burst.

Gus coughed theatrically before speaking.

"I'm due on stage in a minute. We're starting with 'Take Me Home Country Roads'. Make sure you sing along."

Before she could react, Luke turned to help Fliss Fairfax step onto the stage.

Olivia was surprised. And concerned.

"Gus?" she whispered up close. "Is Fliss okay to do this?"

"Of course she is."

"Does she know the song?"

Gus laughed. "Know it? Who do you think I learned it from?"

*

Just after midnight, Olivia took Bella out for a stroll and thought about a wine trip to France. It was six weeks away. A lot could change in six weeks. But what if it didn't? What if her choices remained the same? Would she go? It was all perfectly innocent, of course. She had no plans to get close to Spencer, and he... well, that was the great unknown.

Passing Ken's house, Bella tugged as if wanting to pay a visit. But Ken and Beano would be asleep.

"We'll see them tomorrow," said Olivia, stroking Bella's head.

She supposed that passing Ken's house with Bella would always have them stop like this, either going or coming back. Bella would look for her friend, expecting him to come out and pat her and hand over a treat. And he would do just that, for as long as the Great Unknown allowed.

"Come on, doggie."

Under the full moon, they continued on their way down Colshot Lane.

40

Departures

On a sunny, September morning, Olivia shuffled in her seat and glanced at a Departure Lounge clock. The flight to Nice wouldn't be called for at least another forty minutes. Still, no rush. Not so long ago, she would never have contemplated going to the South of France to house-sit in Provence. But a small-ish chateau near Fréjus in the Provence-Alpes-Côte d'Azur region would be a good place to get an understanding of how the French did things. The fact that scenic Provence was renowned for its rosé wines, fabulous weather, and a dash of style... well, that would be just lovely.

Five days away...

She glanced in the direction of the coffee bar.

Five days in Fréjus – or as history fan Spencer preferred in an exchange of emails, Forum Julii, after Julius Caesar founded a Roman naval base there a couple of thousand years ago.

The weather was glorious. For a second year running,

summer had no intention of finishing early. Back at Whitman Farm, acidity levels were dropping, sugar levels were rising… and the vineyard year was almost complete. She couldn't wait for harvest time in three to four weeks.

Going forward, she was also looking forward to Level Three wine classes starting in October. And she'd spoken with Viv and three others about creating a 'Vibrant Vineyards of Kent' brand for a selection of their wines.

Of course, there were other things going on in Kent. That evening, there would be a parish council meeting. Item One on the agenda was Sue being formally co-opted as a council member. It seemed Son of Colin had never been a popular choice; just that, sometimes, small numbers had the loudest voices.

Then there was the team of professionals and volunteers that the developer, the district council, Sue, Olivia, and Luke were assembling to dismantle the bridge and rebuild it as part of a new pedestrian and cycle route between Forest Edge and the heart of Maybrook. Even the parish council were endorsing it with a cash grant.

Naming it 'Curtis-Fisher Way' had been dealt with. Luke had spoken to Sue to suggest that once the pathway was completed, she might propose a public competition to name it. Katy had already agreed to support her – and to keep quiet for now. They expected to gain a majority for the competition idea. According to Luke, having Alan Curtis-Fisher claiming he'd only agreed to the pathway because he'd secretly arranged to have it named after him… well, the entire village and internet might see that as pathetic, egotistical, and shabby.

As for Ken, he looked his age but was coping with the aid of a home help and everyone mucking in. Olivia was, of course, a regular visitor. She owed him so much. Thankfully, Beano was happy enough with the new arrangements.

As for Sue and Cam – their usually settled existence was a little busier with Bella staying over.

In the lounge at Whitman Farm, six newly framed photos adorned the walls. One was a selfie of Olivia and Bella on the old bridge. Another was of Sue, Milo and Olivia taken at the wedding…

Ah, here he comes…

France would be great. Gail would have been fun, but this was a better alternative.

"I still can't believe that T-shirt," Olivia complained.

"Hey, don't knock Iron Maiden," said Gus, handing her one of the coffees he'd bought.

She smiled – the third newly framed photo in the lounge was of Gus, Olivia and Luke outside the garage. She'd enjoyed putting them all up – and not just because they added a bit of interest to the walls. The fourth was of Ken and Beano among the vines. The fifth photo was a little older – Alice on her 21st birthday. This hung beside her mum, Gloria and another old photo – the musicians.

Olivia sipped her coffee as Gus sat down beside her. Perhaps he didn't look the part, but he *was* the right man.

"You love the T-shirt really, don't you," he said. "I can always spot jealousy."

"Thank God Hannah and Spencer aren't here to see it," said Olivia, wondering how those two were getting on at a vineyard in Bordeaux that Gail's contact had been happy to offer to a teaching professional and her student.

Of course, Gus's pride meant he was going to France on a *quid pro quo* basis. Olivia was paying for the trip. In return, he was paying for their day out to a vintage car rally in East Sussex. She didn't mind at all. The all-new future of Gus's business premises offered an opportunity for him to sort things out for the long term.

"Oh, Luke texted," he said.

"From school?"

"It's break time. He wishes us a safe journey and said we have his permission to hold hands."

Olivia and Luke… they had known each other just over three months, but it felt so much longer. Her focus had been on helping him, but – just occasionally – it gave her a glimpse of what might have been with Jamie.

Luke had decided he would go to university at eighteen. Not local though. An adventure. Somewhere a few hundred miles away – no offence. Until then, he would split his time between Whitman Farm and Beth.

"So," Olivia said, her thoughts turning from England to France. "Fréjus lies south of the Estérel Massif, southwest of Cannes, and is home to a 1st Century amphitheatre, an aqueduct, and ancient fortifications."

"I googled it too," said Gus. "You missed out the bit where it says Fréjus is now a major tourist base with restaurants, beaches and yachts.'

"Well, something for everyone then," said Olivia.

"Thanks," said Gus.

"For this?"

"Yes, for this… and for being so patient with Luke."

"Oh… honestly, it's no problem at all. Quite the opposite. I love spending time with him."

"I know. I find it difficult to be a parent. I never intended it to happen."

"Gus, you do a great job. You really do."

"I admire you, Liv. You're a natural."

Olivia was taken aback.

Gus took her hand.

"I'm surprised you never became a mother," he said. "You would have been brilliant."

She thought of Jamie.

"That's a nice thing to say. Thank you."

"Will you marry me?" he asked.

"What? Oh... yes. Yes, I will. Yes... but not in an Iron Maiden T-shirt."

"You seem to have something in your eye, Liv."

He leaned across from his seat and put his arm around her... and she melted into his embrace, trying to take it all in.

Olivia and Gus... Mr and Mrs... she almost laughed. And Luke...

She and Luke were firm friends now. The arrangements weren't a million percent perfect, but they would all do their best. It was about being on hand when needed and providing him with a space of his own as required. She'd even heard him chatting happily on the phone to a friend the other day. "I'm staying at Olivia's. No, she's not my girlfriend. She's kind of... my stepmother." Her heart had almost burst with joy at that.

Luke had obviously known his dad would be proposing. That pleased her. She would be a kind of part-time, informal step-mum but one with complete commitment, compassion and all the love she could give. And she was very, very happy with that.

"The weather looks good," said Gus. "I can't wait to get there."

"When we're there," said Olivia, a little hesitantly. "When we get a moment... a quiet moment... perhaps when the sun is setting..."

"Yes?"

"I'd like to tell you about Jamie."

The End

257

Thank you for reading Olivia Holmes Meets Luke and Alice. I really hope you enjoyed it. If so, it would be wonderful if you could leave a review on Amazon. As you may know, I don't have a giant publishing house behind me, so your support genuinely makes a difference.

To keep up to date, make sure you sign up for my email newsletter. It only goes out when there's something worth mentioning, such as news about new releases. Simply visit my website where you'll find a straightforward 'Join Newsletter' button.

www.markdaydy.co.uk

Thank you!
Mark

Printed in Great Britain
by Amazon